TROUBLE & STRIFE

TROUBLE & STRIFE

Killer Crime Stories Inspired by Cockney Rhyming Slang

EDITED BY SIMON WOOD

DOWN & OUT BOOKS

Compilation copyright © 2019 by Simon Wood
Story copyrights © 2019 by Individual Authors

All rights reserved. No part of the book may be reproduced in any form or by any electronic or mechanical means, including information storage and retrieval systems, without permission in writing from the publisher, except by a reviewer who may quote brief passages in a review.

Down & Out Books
3959 Van Dyke Road, Suite 265
Lutz, FL 33558
DownAndOutBooks.com

The characters and events in this book are fictitious. Any similarity to real persons, living or dead, is coincidental and not intended by the author.

Cover design by Zach McCain

ISBN: 1-64396-056-3
ISBN-13: 978-1-64396-056-2

CONTENTS

Introduction *Simon Wood*	1
Babbling Brook *Steve Brewer*	3
Bunsen Burner *Angel Luis Colón*	11
Dicky Dirt *Johnny Shaw*	25
Mr. Kipper *Paul Finch*	41
Half Inch *Jay Stringer*	79
Barnet Fair *Catriona McPherson*	93
Tea Leaf *Susanna Calkins*	113
Lee Marvin *Travis Richardson*	129
Trouble And Strife *Colin Campbell*	145
Lady from Bristol *Sam Wiebe*	161
Pleasure and Pain *Robert Dugoni*	169
About the Contributors	199

INTRODUCTION
Simon Wood

I love colorful language. The sheer creativity of subverting our day to day speech is something I enjoy. That's the essence of slang. Every culture uses slang where people throw away the formality of language to convey an emotion or a situation in a succinct phrase. In my opinion, no other slang form is more enjoyable than Cockney rhyming slang where rhyme is incorporated.

So what is Cockney rhyming slang? It's essentially a code. You take a word, replace that word with a word that rhymes with it, then turn it into a phrase.

Example: the word 'Look.' Look rhymes 'hook.' Turn 'hook' into a phrase and you get 'butcher's hook.' *Butcher's hook* is a classic cockney rhyming slang for look.

Other classic rhyming slang phrases include:
Dog and bone…meaning phone.
Holy water…meaning daughter.
Plates of meat…meaning feet.
Sky rocket…meaning pocket.

If you're really clever with your rhyming slang, it can be an ironic phrase for the original word, like with 'Trouble and strife' which is rhyming slang for 'wife.'

Now the fun doesn't stop there. Oh no! Invariably, to incorporate your rhyming slang into a sentence, you would drop the rhyming word and just say Butcher's instead of Butcher's Hook. So if someone said to you, "Give me a *Butcher's*?" then the person would be asking to have a look at something in your possession.

So what are the origins of Cockney rhyming slang? It originated out of London's East End in the mid-1900s and was supposedly used by criminals to prevent undercover cops from listening in on their conversations. Like many things in British culture, that explanation has been disputed. While there are several other similar explanations, none seem definitive. The only concrete information is when, where and by whom.

Cockney rhyming slang still flourishes over a hundred and fifty years later. It's no longer restricted to a particular enclave of London. It's part of the national lexicon with regional differences and the incorporation of modern references have superseded many traditional phrases, such as 'Chevy Chase' overtaking 'Boat race' for meaning 'face.'

The thing I love about Cockney rhyming slang is that the phrases paint colorful pictures. My favorite rhyming slang is the 'Gypsy's Kiss." That creates such an imaginative visual of the story behind those two evocative words...although we should ignore that it's actually slang for 'piss.' It was the evocativeness of Cockney rhyming slang that I wanted to use for this anthology. I wanted these colorful phrases to inspire the contributors to come up with a story. I chose writers from both the US and the UK to exploit their familiarity and unfamiliarity with the rhyming slang.

To see what they came up with, turn the page and have a *butcher's*.

BABBLING BROOK
Inspired by the Rhyming Slang for Crook
Steve Brewer

"I've always had the gift of gab," Sammy Kelso said. "That's why they assign the new guys to bunk in here with me. I'm the Welcome Wagon for the state penitentiary."

Sammy laughed, but he couldn't tell whether his new cellmate joined in. They were in their bunks, Sammy staring up at the underside of the steel shelf that served as the new guy's bed. Past lights out, but it was never completely dark in the cell. Always some light filtering in from the corridor, where guards strolled the night away.

"Judging from the ink on your arms," Sammy said, "you've been inside before. This prison works pretty much like all the others, but I'm happy to answer any questions you might have."

He paused, but no sound came from the top bunk. Sammy wondered whether his cellmate had drifted off. It took a minute to remember the new guy's name, but then it came to him.

"Jesse?" he whispered. "You awake?"

The new guy grunted.

"I can stop talking if you're ready to sleep."

"No," Jesse said. "Go ahead."

Sammy thought he'd better clear the air right away. Before this young man got the wrong idea.

"Listen," he said, "I'm a big talker, but you should know I never talk to the authorities. Some places, they bunk a new guy with a snitch. But it's not like that here. Anything we say is just between the two of us."

"Good."

"So you can speak freely," Sammy said. "I find that it's not talkative people you have to worry about. It's the quiet ones, the ones who are always listening and judging. Those are the ones who will stab you in the back."

"Hmm."

"There are exceptions, of course, especially when it comes to women. A chatty redhead is the reason I've been inside the past fifteen years."

The new guy said nothing, but Sammy needed no prompting.

"Most species of rat—your snitches, your undercover operatives—are the quiet type. They keep their ears open and their mouths shut. But not this woman. She never stopped talking. She couldn't help it. For her, talking was a nervous disorder, a twitch."

"What did she talk about?"

"Anything," Sammy said. "*Everything.* A song she heard on the radio. Some show she watched on TV. Celebrity gossip. Stories about her friends and *their* friends. It never stopped. Her name was Brook, so we called her Babbling Brook."

"To her face?"

"No, man, that would've been rude. Whenever she wasn't around. She was dating one of the guys in my crew, though, so she was kinda always around."

"And she was a rat?"

"Worse," Sammy said. "She was an undercover cop."

"Oof. You never suspected her?"

"Not for a minute," Sammy said. "I was on alert for the quiet types like her boyfriend. Kinda shy, always hanging back. That's probably why it was easy for her to sink her claws into him. The guy's shy, he's lonely, and here's this chatty babe who's his exact opposite."

"What was his name?"

"Rocky. A nickname from when he was a kid, but he never grew into it. He was kinda skinny and nerdy. Wore glasses."

"Was he a cop, too?"

"No, no. Just a lovelorn sap."

Jesse snorted.

"We were planning this great heist," Sammy said. "Rocky was supposed to handle the electronics—your burglar alarms, your surveillance cameras, what have you. I didn't really know him, but the other guy in the crew, Nick, vouched for him and I'd known Nick since high school. We met in shop class, both of us making zip-guns instead of the assigned project."

Sammy laughed at the memory from forty years ago. Young Jesse didn't seem like much of a laugher. But he wasn't snoring, either, so Sammy told him the rest of the well-worn story.

"We'd gotten word of a sweet setup at the recycling plant west of Albuquerque, out in the desert."

"Recycling?"

"It's where the garbage trucks take everything from the blue recycling bins—your aluminum and your plastics and every kind of paper. The trucks dump it in this huge yard, where it gets sorted by people and by this conveyor system that uses magnets to separate out the metals—"

"You robbed a *trash* place?"

"I was skeptical, too, at first. But the more Nick told us about it, the more it looked like a big haul if we hit 'em on payday. Most people who work as sorters are homeless or they're fresh out of jail. They don't have bank accounts, so they're paid in cash."

"Ah."

"The recycling company kept the payroll in a safe overnight. They also used the safe to hold anything valuable the sorters turned up in the trash, from rare metals to gold teeth."

Sammy paused to catch his breath.

"We spent three weeks studying the place, figuring out their routines and where the payroll was kept. We stayed in this rental house on the west side, poring over maps and making plans. The whole time, Babbling Brook hung around the fringes, making drinks, yakking her head off. More than once, I had to go for a walk around the neighborhood to hear myself think."

"Why didn't you make her stay away?"

"Exactly what we should've done," Sammy said. "But it was awkward, with her being Rocky's new girl. And she acted like our heist plans were fascinating, batting her eyes and tossing her red hair, so we all were guilty of telling her too much. You know how men are. Women make us soft in the head."

"Been there," Jesse said.

"Anyway, the day of the heist, she shows up at the recycling plant with Rocky."

"You didn't know she'd be there?"

"No! Rocky was in the lead vehicle, arriving right at dawn. As soon as he disabled the alarms and got the front gate open, he sent us a text and we came roaring up the gravel road in a van. We were already inside the fence before we saw her sitting in Rocky's car.

"Me and Nick nearly shat ourselves, but it was too late to turn back. We tied up the security guard and broke into the office, which was a little mobile home landscaped to look like a real building. The safe was bolted to the wall, but it's a trailer, so the wall's only about three inches thick.

"Nick had a portable cutting torch, and he started cutting the wall around the safe. We were going to pop it out of the exterior wall and put it in the van and drive away. We figured we could take our time cracking the safe once we got away from there."

"Good plan," Jesse said.

"Except for the cop in our midst. While we were busy

prying that safe out of the wall, Babbling Brook was calling in the cavalry. By the time we got it loaded into the van, four police cars were zooming up the road."

He fell silent as a guard passed in the corridor, heels thudding on the tile floor. Once the sound faded away, Sammy said, "Nick wanted to make a break for it, but Brook drew down on him with this little pistol. Said she was the police and we were all under arrest."

"Bold."

"I know, right? Three against one."

"She had reinforcements coming."

"Yeah, but still. Nick was having none of it. He pulled a pistol out of his belt and they started shooting at each other. Brook hit Nick a couple of times, but they were small-caliber bullets and they barely staggered a big guy like him. Meanwhile, he was blasting away with a .45. Shot her right in her pretty face."

A long silence, then Jesse said, "What did you do?"

"I froze. I was so surprised, I couldn't process the whole thing. First, there's a woman at the job who's not supposed to be there. Next thing you know, she's a cop and she's shooting at Nick. Then she's dead and the sirens are getting close."

"So what happened?"

"Rocky was pretty upset with Nick for shooting his girlfriend, even if she had turned out to be a rat. He pulled out a pistol, too, though he seemed to be in a daze. He pointed it at Nick like his arm was moving on its own accord.

"I said, 'No, no, no,' but it was too late. He and Nick both pulled their triggers. It was like the guns went 'bang' right together. They both went down, dying. And there I stood, in shock, as the cops surrounded us."

"Last man standing," Jesse said.

"I never pulled my piece out of my pocket, but they treated me like a cop killer. I'll never see the outside world again. Not in this lifetime."

The men chewed on that for a minute, then Jesse said, "They held you responsible."

"That's what they said," Sammy said. "But I was there for a simple robbery. The shooting took me by surprise. And it was over in less than a minute."

"A minute that changed everything."

"You got that right."

Another silence. Sammy was beginning to think his new cellmate had finally dozed off when Jesse said, "I knew I'd hear this story someday, from your own lips."

"What's that?" Sammy leaned out a little, squinting, but he couldn't see the man in the upper bunk.

"Everybody on the inside knows the story," Jesse said. "You've been telling it for fifteen years."

"It was the pivotal moment in my life. It's bound to come up in conversation."

Sammy snaked a hand inside his orange jumpsuit and scratched his chest. The scar from an old knife wound often itched and tingled, though it had healed a decade ago.

"I had a moment like that, too," Jesse said. "When I was a kid, I lost someone close to me. After that, my life went off the rails. Drugs, booze, shoplifting, the usual. I've been in and out of stir since I was fifteen."

"So you're an old hand at—"

"I know how to work the system. Who to pressure. Who to pay off. You can get what you want if you work it hard enough."

"Yeah?" Sammy said. "And what is it that you want?"

"To be right here. In this cell. At this moment."

"Is that some kind of Zen thing? Because I don't—"

Jesse suddenly dropped out of the top bunk, soundless as a panther in his bare feet. He leaned in at Sammy, his teeth and eyes gleaming. Sammy tried to scoot away, but he was up against the concrete wall. Jesse lunged at him, stuffing a rolled-up pair of white socks into Sammy's gaping mouth.

As Sammy gagged on the dry socks, Jesse punched him twice in the face. *Bap, bap.* The blows made him see stars. He could feel Jesse's breath on his face as the younger man pressed him down with his powerful arms.

"My turning point," Jesse growled, "was the same one as yours."

He wrapped his hands around Sammy's throat.

"The person I lost? She was my big sister. The one person in the world I could trust. She was a cop. And her name was Brook."

Sammy thrashed and bucked, but it had no effect on the angry young man. Meanwhile, Sammy's right hand scrabbled frantically along the wall, searching the edge of the mattress. He felt close to blacking out, but his fingers finally found the four-inch-long shiv he'd fashioned from a sharpened shard of steel.

Sammy stabbed blindly at his cellmate, the short blade hitting him in the ribs and the back and the gut. Jesse let go of his throat, but Sammy kept stabbing at him. Hot blood spritzed across the bunk.

They rolled off onto the concrete floor, Sammy landing on top. He scooped the socks out of his mouth and took a ragged gasp of air as he pinned Jesse to the floor with his full weight.

Jesse coughed, dark blood staining his teeth. Sammy sank the shiv into the side of his neck, into the soft spot just below his ear, and Jesse went still.

Sammy caught his breath for a minute before he climbed up to sit on the edge of his blood-spattered bunk. His voice was raspy as he called for a guard.

A fat sergeant named Hernandez appeared at the door. He shined his flashlight into the cell and the beam roamed over the bloody corpse. He shouted for other guards to call an ambulance, then he opened the cell door.

"Jesus Christ, what happened, Sammy?"

"Kid came at me with a shiv. I took it away from him, but

he kept fighting me, so I used it on him."

"You sure did. He's not going to need that ambulance."

"Stupid punk," Sammy said. "He thought he'd make a splash on his first night in the pen, show everybody he was tough. He hadn't counted on running into an old lifer with nothing to lose."

Hernandez nodded. They'd seen this sort of Wild West behavior before.

"You hurt?"

"I'm all right," Sammy said. "Soon as you guys get him out of here, I'll get some clean sheets and go back to bed."

"Just like that," Hernandez said. "You kill a man, then you go to sleep like nothing happened."

"I need my rest for whoever the warden sends next."

"He does keep sending you the hard cases."

"I don't mind being the Welcome Wagon," Sammy said. "It helps pass the time."

BUNSEN BURNER
Inspired by the Rhyming Slang for Earner
Angel Luis Colón

"Jesus, Teddy, the fuck are you doing here?" Louis Fourteen—called that on account of the fact he looked like puberty swung its bat and missed him by a wide berth—stared at me with unblinking eyes. "How the hell are you not in hiding?"

"What?" Best question I had in me after one sip of coffee.

I was twenty minutes away from a warm bed and hours away from a fifth of whiskey. Said whiskey was much closer and left a film on my memory. I lost track of the world in a cab on the way back to my apartment. No way could I fuck things up with my boss in that span of time.

Louis shook his head. "You got The Lady Cosh pissed, my friend. You done fucked up."

I took a long sip of weak coffee. "No clue what you're talking about." I tried to bring the last hours of drunkenness back to the front of my mind, but it was no use. Hell, that I made it into my apartment and into my bed with keys, wallet, and phone accounted for were minor fucking miracles.

Louis sighed. "Figured they was burying your ass in Staten Island the way I heard it."

I stared at Louis for a beat. "You gonna tell me what it is I did? Or do I get to keep hearing all this vague bullshit pour out of your mouth?"

Louis licked his lips. "Fuck if I know. All I heard was you pissed her off and now she's raising hell from across the Atlantic to anyone who'll listen about stringing you up and treating you like a piñata."

"Those were her exact words?"

"Maybe. You know how she gets. Remember Bobby No-Toes?"

"Considering Cosh was why he had no toes, yes, yes I do remember Bobby No-Toes."

I fought the urge to box Louie's ears. Hazy memories of using my phone made me fish it out of my pocket to check the call history. Nothing past 11:50 p.m.—I was still drinking then. "Look," I said as I thumbed further and further back into my call history, as if something from four days ago would provide clarity, "Who told you this?"

"You know damn well the only one of us she's calling directly is Benny," Louie said, "Anyone else hears her voice on the other end of the line and they know they're fucked."

The Lady Cosh had a reputation—I mean, any reasonable crime boss did—but hers was a very different story. Ran drugs out of Ireland for decades. Literally on life eight of nine by most accounts. I never met her personally but most fellas who did talked about a frail woman who dressed impeccably and was scarred head to toe. Most stories were different when it came to the circumstance, but everyone knew that she managed to literally crawl out of a five-alarm fire of her own free will after being trapped for nearly twenty minutes.

The Lady Cosh had no business being alive.

They said her nerves were fried, that she didn't feel any pain. That was supposed to be what made her such a stone-cold piece of shit. I didn't believe that entirely but still felt my stomach tighten at the thought of that woman's anger being aimed my way. There was no direct proof, but I'd heard of plenty of people magically disappearing after fucking her over.

Some said she personally flew their asses out to Ireland to torture and kill them. Others said she didn't bother with that shit, she just had her personal enforcer end the drama with two bullets to the skull.

Neither option seemed pleasant.

"Benny said this?" I wanted confirmation. Louis and Benny were the town gossips. They also loved busting balls and man, if this was a prank, I was ready to bite their goddamn noses off their pasty faces. Benny was also my in-between man. He was the guy who lined up my jobs. I thought we were close, but if he was telling anyone who would listen that I had an appointment with a Glock, then there wasn't much hope.

"Yep." The idiot didn't follow up. Gave me a 'yep' like I was asking if there was any food in the fridge.

"And where the fuck is he, Louis? Jesus, it's like pulling teeth with you this morning."

"I'm tired."

"I'm hung-fucking-over but you don't see me seizing up like a broken lawnmower. Words, man, use them."

"Fine, fine. Benny's out at the Knights of Columbus on Middletown. Think they're doing some work on the walls there. Couple of guys got into a scrap last night. Heard someone ended up tasting drywall."

"And Benny's there all day? I'm not gonna take a cab for nothing, right?"

"Nah, he's the only one knows how to hang drywall—he'll be there."

"Great, thanks." I walked away feeling like I was trying to keep my head above flood water.

Benny was sitting at the back of the bar in the Knights of Columbus reading a newspaper. His fingers were caked with dried plaster. He wiped his palms on his lap and frowned at me as I walked in. "Hey," he said. "You mind grabbing me one of those rags over there?" Benny pointed to the opposite end of the bar where the sink was.

I grabbed a wet rag and tossed it over. "Louis says Cosh is pissed at me." No point in beating around the bush.

Benny caught the rag and scrubbed his hands as clean as he could. "What I heard."

"Any idea why? Didn't I just sort out that cash flow problem with the jackets? She got triple back on that deal and no static with the Albanians or the cops."

"You know the business." Benny inspected his fingernails.

"The fuck is going on with you assholes today?" I rubbed my eyes. "That I'm breathing means you're all fucking with me or this isn't as bad as I think it is."

"Oh, it's pretty fucking bad."

"How is it bad?"

"Brother," Benny said as he finally made eye contact with me, "She's coming stateside to deal with you directly. Nobody's supposed to touch you until she's touched you."

I couldn't afford a flight. No credit and not enough available cash to get me anywhere safe. A train or a bus was a solid choice but then I'd still be in trouble wherever I ended up—I had no goddamn job skills past punching things or people. A loser; that is what I was, a loser who helped better people hold onto their money and power. A loser so bad at that job that his boss' boss was on her way to personally rip his fucking head off—the least drastic thing I could imagine Cosh doing to me.

I thought about the night in question. Thought about the beer and the last-minute shots at the bar. The laughter. I thought about the girls at the end of the bar that I was too far gone to make even the saddest attempt at a pick-up. The memories were mottled, though. Little glimpses of conversation and people but nothing out of the ordinary. The drinking was good and loud. The laughter was in surplus—a good night, hell, a great night.

Too great of a night.

I sat on the edge of my bed staring at an empty book bag. Two- or three-days' worth of clothes. I'd be hungry before I started to stink wherever I went. I needed to pull in cash and I needed it hours ago. I needed to dip into my work life and make another mistake to get out of the mistake I made the night before. I checked my phone again, as if the fortieth time I checked would reveal a late-night phone call to Ireland. I checked around my apartment too. Looked for notes, anything that could point to a fuck-up. I found a half-empty pack of cheap cigarettes on the floor near my dresser. Branding on the package wasn't even in English. I rarely smoked, though. Checked my clothes and they didn't stink.

These weren't my cigarettes.

I crouched down and lowered my head to get an eyeful of dust bunnies, loose change, and something else I knew wasn't mine: a flip phone. I grabbed the ancient tech and opened it. Held the power button until the screen lit up a sickly hue of yellow and the carrier's name faded into a pixilated menu of call options.

Recent calls.

By instinct, I touched the screen and rolled my eyes when nothing happened. I dragged my thumb down to the keypad and relearned how to navigate something that only ten years back was second nature to me. A little wheel appeared and changed colors before the list of recent calls showed up. At the top of the list, an outbound call at 3:21 a.m. to one LADY COSH.

And that's when I remembered—well, mostly remembered.

I remembered tattoos. I didn't remember exactly what they were of or how many there were, but the bastard was covered in them. Even had ink on his scalp—whatever I could see of it since he was growing in a fine layer of scruff. Had a patchy beard too. He was loud—jovial loud—but also seemed paranoid enough to stare over his shoulder every couple of words.

Irish. Off-the-boat lilt—probably from somewhere out west, close to the coast. He had moments where his accent went indecipherable. He worked at being understood, though. He worked at being my bar friend that night—overtime, even.

This meant shots. Lots and lots of shots.

No names exchanged. Just laughter and random stories of stupid things done to us or others. I talked a big game about my collection racket—about how good I was at making fellas sweat before paying out. I took pride in the fact that I only ever broke a few fingers. Never had to drop a body behind the horse track or at a Staten Island junkyard. I had a clean record. Worst I'd ever get locked up for was intimidation or whatever.

"Extortion," the Irishman told me, "Yer hands keep clean but then it's all white-collar stuff, right? Fuck with someone's money and they'll put you away for longer than they would for taking a finger or a toe."

"What do you do?" I think I asked.

"Me? A chemist. I mix volatile things together, add a naked flame," he clapped his hands shut and then pulled them apart slowly, "Boom."

I remember being confused but not what I said in reply to the Irishman. It wasn't important—maybe. The conversation jumped all over the place and we talked sports, we talked women, we talked family. All the bullshit two nightlong friends will ever speak about before forgetting about each other forever.

Alcohol's a hell of an eraser.

The night wasn't just drinking. No, we went elsewhere. We walked someplace, and I knew we walked because I remembered the biting cold—it was that first mean January night that always came the week after New Year's in the city. Not like it wasn't cold before, but there's always that first night where it feels like Mother Nature gave the fuck up and ditched. So, we walked for a little. Then a cab? We had to have gone to my apartment because the cigarettes and the phone did not belong to me.

No, they belonged to the Irish chemist.

He goaded me.

"Get on with it, yah yellow-bellied fucker," he said holding the phone to my face, "Just fucking ask. Ask the goddamn question and we're golden. Be a pal." The cigarette hanging out of his mouth stank to high hell.

There was a question from him and there was apprehension from me—fear. He wanted me to call Cosh but why? What the fuck did he want with Cosh and why did he choose me? Did I give him the number in the first place? I was low-level, I mean, yes, she knew who I was—I made sure she got her money—but I wasn't essential. I wasn't a big name on the list, a person someone from the FBI would agonize over arresting or questioning. Still, the Irishman wanted me to do the talking. He wanted me to take the blame.

Apparently, I did. I couldn't remember what I said, and that was the real problem. That was why I needed to run and keep a low profile for a long time. Nobody in New York loved me enough to miss me and anyone related to me would be glad to see me gone.

I was sweating this for far too long. The cigarettes, the phone, and the Irish chemist didn't matter. Nothing was going to solve the problem of having one of most vicious women to live dirty come at me like a fox terrier going for a toddler's fingers. I gathered what was mine—pocketed that extra phone in case—and left my apartment.

I needed traveling money and the only available place to make a withdrawal was my day job. Now that was a dumb idea—taking Cosh's money—but I was already in trouble. I got my bag, got my coat, and locked up the apartment for the last time.

***

Guy by the name of Hector Figueroa frequented a dance club just a block away from my apartment. He owed Cosh three large, not a massive amount, but considering he was a few weeks behind, the vig probably jacked that total up a little closer to five. That amount could get me the fuck out of New York in a bus and far enough away to hide at a no-tell-motel for a week or two while I found work. Now, realistically? I'd be lucky to get a few hundred out of the guy running an ambush at a dance club, but it would still get me further than the few dollars I had in my pocket.

The club was called Sidestreet, conveniently located, well, on a side street near the train station. This meant it was easy to get to and easy to get the hell away from after I made my collection. For a moment, I wondered if Hector would disappoint me by not showing, but I knew better. Men like Hector were creatures of habit and they worked hard to fund those habits. Debt was something that lived next to them, always threatening to cut them off at the knees, but that was what made it worth it: that thrill, that feeling anything could come crashing down at any time.

Hector loved dancing at this club; therefore, he was dancing at this club.

The guys at the door knew me well. They'd let me in knowing a few twenties would come their way as I made an exit. Did wonders for their memory loss whenever cops came around asking questions. Probably wouldn't help as much if Cosh or one of her main men showed up, but it would get me out the door and onto a train. I could go straight to Port Authority and hop onto the first goddamn Greyhound leaving the state. Maybe Ohio. Nobody from Europe would ever go to fucking Ohio.

I wasn't necessarily dressed for the club, but that wasn't a problem. The boys at the door had that glimmer in their eyes—the hope of a little extra cash on what looked to be a quiet night spurring their kindness.

Me, I took it in stride. "How's it going fellas?" I gave each monster a handshake like I was on the fucking campaign trail.

I got a chorus of 'good' and 'a'ight' as a reply. A firm pat on the shoulder as I walked by—a friendly reminder that I was walking by guys with enough height and strength to do me grievous bodily harm. That harm wasn't close to the shit I'd heard about Cosh getting into, so the risk was justified.

The club was nearly empty. A few girls were dancing along with whatever the house band was playing. The bartenders stood at their posts looking bored. A few tables were occupied by some young idiots with more money to spend on clothes than they had brain cells. They all leaned on their tables; heads swimming with that cocaine buzz from their third- or fourth-bathroom visit.

Hector was stationed near the DJ booth—cat named Henry Knowles busy with prep for when the band was finished. I liked Henry, so I gave him a little nod as I walked over. Henry caught my eye and walked off like a goddamn pro. He knew damn well the shit Hector got into and he knew damn well the shit I got into. Henry wasn't a fan of mixing chemicals, so he walked off before Hector noticed I was coming.

"Look at my man living his best life." I always liked opening warm. It was better than coming in too hot. Adrenaline made assholes brave and Hector was enough of an asshole to become a fucking superhero if I set him off. The goal was to get him to part with his cash quick. Worst case: I threw a punch or two. Put the fear of me into Hector enough to pull the scratch out of his pocket and then run my ass over to the train before things got weird.

Hector extended a hand and I took it.

"Shit, man, you coming at dudes on their downtime?" he smirked.

"City don't sleep and neither do the working men," I replied.

"That some low-key shade?"

"No sun in here, is there?" I stepped a little closer, edging into the personal space to let my size do some talking too. "You know why I'm here."

"They said I had another week." Hector fiddled with the straw in his drink.

"Not up to me to question the old lady."

Hector stared off to the side and sighed. "Fine." He reached into his front jacket pocket and pulled out a bill fold. "This should tide her over. I can cover the rest next week."

I took the money. I learned a long time ago to never question a man when the money's there to take. "Smartest man I ever met, Hector. That's why people like you."

Hector nodded. "You gonna count that? I probably owe another two on top of it."

"Then I'll trust that. You did me a favor in not needing to get messy about any of this." I extended a hand. I wanted Hector to feel as good as he could about losing this money. Pretty sure he wasn't going to feel great when it came time for him to pay his true debt. Didn't matter. Hector was an idiot and sometimes idiots had to learn their lessons.

I sure as hell was learning mine.

Money collected, I stepped out of the club and dispensed a little scratch to the doormen before that sinking feeling settled in and my greed outran my wisdom. I booked it to the train and managed to slip between closing doors in the nick of time. The car was packed, but I found a nice spot between two people who didn't smell like the rankest part of a garbage truck. Once we were past 138th Street and underground, I felt all that pressure fade away. I reminded myself that was never a good way to confront a bad situation; that any moment this train could stop and in would walk Cosh or one of her goons to end me. They could be waiting for me at the bus station too. I was leaving a mess behind and sooner or later someone would come to clean up. Didn't matter how far I ran. I needed to remember that—this wasn't a one-night decision, it was for life.

I kept looking over my shoulder with those thoughts in

mind. There was no safety. There was just a little burst of quiet. I couldn't let myself feel like this was over—even when I was over state lines. Even years later. I needed to be vigilant and be miserable forever because that was the life I chose. I decided to call it a penance, a means of making up for years of bringing misery into other people's lives. It was a good way to rationalize all this shit. It kept me from jumping face first into a pity party that would leave me in the kind of mental state a person needs to be in to quit. I saw that enough times during my collection runs. There was always someone ready to quit—ready to take life on the chin instead of doing something.

Port Authority was packed with people, but nobody gave me a second look. I bought a cheap bus ticket to Columbus, Ohio. A late-night ride that would get me into town around 3:30 a.m. I decided to figure out what to do when I got there—no need to sweat the details until it was necessary. Maybe I'd wait for another bus and go further west. Maybe I'd stay right there and become a nothing man in a nothing place. Didn't matter until the choice was there to make.

The phone in my inside pocket rang. Not my phone. The burner phone.

I jerked up from my seat. Was lucky enough to get the set all to myself because only five other assholes were traveling to Ohio the same time as I was. I looked out the window and we were at a gas station. Car next to us had Pennsylvania plates. I looked at my watch and it looked like we were only two hours into the drive. Couldn't understand why the bus had to stop unless someone was whining for a bathroom—cheap bus meant no toilet.

I pulled the phone from my pocket. That tiny screen on the front said, UNKNOWN CALLER. I didn't open it. I looked up and realized nobody was on the bus. The lights weren't on and it seemed the engine wasn't either. The phone stopped ringing.

"Ohio wouldn't be far enough," a raspy, drained voice from behind me said. "Smarter man would go north. Maybe Canada, maybe Nova Scotia. Nobody ever goes to Nova Scotia." Once upon a time, there was an accent there, but the life was drained out of this voice. It felt like something spoke to me from the other side of a tomb.

It was Cosh.

"I was working off instinct," I said.

"And here I thought your instincts were well-seasoned."

I went to turn around. Wanted to look her in the eye when I made my case.

"Bad choice. Eyes ahead, never behind."

I stopped and moved my head back to stare at the back of the seat in front of me.

I smelled cigar smoke.

"Theodore. The man who gave you that phone. Where is he?"

"I don't remember." My voice cracked. "I was blacked out, Lady Cosh, I didn't realize I called you until I found the phone."

Cosh wheezed but didn't say anything.

"I mean, if I knew there was a problem…I wasn't aiming to offend or do anything wrong, you know me. You know I'm faithful."

"But you ran…" she held the 'n' as if she was tasting it. "Ran like a coward as soon as word got out I was on my way. Faithful always comes back, faithful doesn't turn tail."

"I slipped. Got scared. Am I wrong to be scared?"

Cosh made a sound like she was choking—laughter. "I've yet to figure that out. What I do know is that we're not in the business of why. What matters is you made a mistake and then you doubled down on it."

I held up the phone. "If you can use it, take it. I promise I got no idea who it was that did this."

I felt her hand brush mine as she took the phone. The skin was abnormally smooth. The stories about her—about the burns—they must have been true. "Do you remember what you told me?"

"No. No I don't."

"You said, 'Blacky Jaguar says to go fuck yourself.'"

"I have no idea who that is." That was the truth. The name was ridiculous. Didn't sound like anyone in the area or in another crew.

Cosh sighed. "Theodore, I understand this is very confusing but that name, that name, my how it stings me. I've got nobody else to take this out on, understand?"

I shook my head. "I didn't realize it was you until the next day."

"A smarter man would have known from the start. A smarter man would have known better than to drink his mind rotten when surrounded by strangers. What would it say about me, Theodore, if I let that stand? What would it say to others if they knew someone in my crew could be plied with a drink to play a child's prank on me?"

"It's a simple mistake."

"Simple mistakes grow like weeds." Cosh let the words hang a moment. "It took me far too long to learn that."

A pop. Loud. Set my ears ringing almost immediately. All the air left me. I felt like I'd sprinted for a mile, my chest burned so bad. Went cross-eyed for a second before the headrest on the seat in front of me went from three back to one. Couldn't catch my damn breath. Couldn't feel my hands.

The Lady Cosh stood beside me. I turned to her and couldn't make out the details. Felt her smooth hand on mine.

"An example must be made." Cosh dug her other hand into my pockets. She lifted the billfold I got from Hector. "How much does he owe after this?"

I blinked. The math should have been easy. "I…" I licked

my lips; my tongue was so dry. "I think another two or three large. Didn't count." I felt exhausted. All this running—this stress—was wearing me down.

Cosh counted the money. "Three hundred dollars. You trusted too easy, Theodore. Let your desperation blind you." She placed a hand on my head. Her thumb between my eyes. "Now rest boy. You played your part. Rest easy knowing what comes next is not your fault."

The Lady Cosh walked away. I watched her tiny frame disappear from the bus. Nobody came back, and I couldn't catch my damn breath. No matter how deep I breathed, it just wouldn't come back.

DICKY DIRT
Inspired by the Rhyming Slang for Shirt
Johnny Shaw

Ross Hartshorne didn't like Tanya Morgan. He didn't find her attractive. She had stringy hair and dead eyes. Her laugh grated on him and she laughed all the time. At all the wrong things. She had a nasty tongue and could be downright mean. He had once seen her kick a dog. Ross really couldn't stand the woman.

But that didn't mean he wasn't going to have sex with her.

Ross believed in seizing opportunities when they arose. That's how he found himself on a Tuesday night on top of Tanya Morgan pumping away like he was trying to snake a clogged drain.

It had very little to do with her. Nothing really. Her husband, Craig Morgan, had given him a brutal beating twenty years earlier when they were both in the tenth grade. Ross had never avenged the humiliation of that moment, but had thought about it regularly.

Someone famous in some movie once said that revenge is a cold dish. That's the way Ross saw it. The years didn't matter. By banging his wife, Ross was hitting Craig Morgan over the head with a bowl made of ice. But only in a covert way, because if Craig Morgan found out, he would kill Ross. The revenge had to be Ross's secret with himself.

Craig hadn't gotten any saner since high school. To be honest, he was a straight-up psychopath. Getting on his bad side was dangerous. Even Craig's good side could get you hospitalized. He beat the shit out of Doc Proctor just for accidentally playing the wrong song on the jukebox with his quarter. And they're best friends. Although it probably won't be the last time someone got a beat down for playing Mr. Roboto in a desert bar.

Maybe if he had the chance, Ross could tell Craig on his deathbed. Although he didn't really see a scenario where he would be invited to that event.

Whatever the opposite of guilt was, that's what Ross felt. Ross didn't believe in bad choices. What he did was what he did. There wasn't any upside in second guessing something once it was decided. All of Ross's choices were good choices. He didn't make mistakes.

"Are you almost finished?" Tanya said, her voice flat. She stared back at him with those dumb, dead eyes.

"Yeah, I guess. I'm getting a little raw." Ross gave a couple courtesy pumps and rolled off her. He stared at the ceiling, catching his breath. "You're sure Craig won't be back until morning?"

"Probably. He usually stops at the casino when he works in Indio."

"Doesn't matter. I'm going to take off. Unless you want to cuddle."

Tanya stared at him. She found her phone on the nightstand and looked at the screen.

Ross waited for a moment, then got the hint that this interaction was over. He got out of bed and looked for his pants.

"I'm going to have to tell him, you know," Tanya said, matter of fact.

"Tell who? Tell Craig?" Ross said. "Why would you do that?"

"I like it when he gets jealous and hurts people. It feels like he loves me."

***

A week later, Ross wasn't thinking about Tanya or Craig Morgan, other than to occasionally bask in the glow of his secret revenge. The sex had been bad and he had gotten a speeding ticket driving home, but there were no clouds on the horizon. No reason to expect a storm.

Ross put on his best Hawaiian shirt, the one with the images of topless hula dancers, and strolled over to Boog's for their monthly luau. As luaus went, Ross didn't think it was authentic, but he had never been to Hawaii, so he couldn't judge for sure. Cultural accuracy wasn't on his list of reasons for attending. Two-dollar mai tais were high on the list. There were always a couple drunks that ended up putting on the coconut bras and fake grass skirts. And the Mexican that played Don Ho songs in the corner was good, even if he sang all the songs in Spanish.

He dropped a five on the bar and ordered his drinks. Strolling through the small bar, he two-fisted a couple of mai tais in plastic cups. He took sips from each one, making it clear that they were both his. He wanted to get a little more drunk before he socialized, so he posted up near the back door to watch the show. A bunch of desert rats squirm-danced on each other like Axl Rose to Pequeñas Burbujas.

When Craig Morgan walked in the door, Ross involuntarily pooped a little. More like a prairie dog poking its head out and returning to his tunnel, but it counted.

Craig did not look like he was there to party. He looked like he was there to hurt someone. Someone named Ross.

Craig had worked labor jobs most of his life. A body lumped with muscles and an off-putting asymmetry like a hunchback bodybuilder. He wore thick glasses with black frames, his cross-eyes never quite looking at the person in front of him. The vertical indentation between his eyebrows was so thick with hate that it looked like a knife wound.

Before Ross could hide, Craig was halfway across the room heading in his direction. He shoved men and women out of the way, brushing them to the side like they were tall grass.

Tony Alvarez took umbrage at getting shoved and hit Craig with a haymaker across the jaw. It turned Craig's head and his glasses flew off his face and landed somewhere behind the bar.

"Shit" was all Tony Alvarez said before Craig caveman-punched him right on top of the head, buckling Tony's knees and sending him crumpling to the ground.

Ross didn't wait to see the remainder of Tony's fate. He was out the back door and into the night.

The moment Ross stepped into the back patio of Boog's, he remembered that there was no back exit. Three tall stucco walls surrounded him, razor wire at the top because of that time Gweez Rodriguez tried to sneak a cougar into the bar as a gag. There would usually be smokers out back, but all the smokers had migrated to the front after a sewage pipe broke and made the ground swampy and the whole area smell like the dysentery ward of a shitting hospital.

Trapped and frantic, Ross looked for a place to hide. He didn't even consider fighting Craig. The man was a force of nature.

"Hey, Ross."

Ross jumped. Dicky Dirt walked out of the shadows in the far corner. He zipped up his fly, wiped his hands on his pants, and reached out to shake. Ross took his hand out of instinct. It was wet.

"Dicky Dirt," Ross said.

"Nobody calls me that no more. Only you call me that."

Dicky Dirt had been in Ross's class in grade school all the way through high school. He had been skinny as a kid, but had filled out, about the same size as Ross now. He wasn't much to look at, his only distinguishing feature his huge Adam's apple.

Ross glanced at the backdoor, knowing that at any moment it was going to fly off its hinges and Craig was going to rhino-charge him.

"That's a pretty sweet shirt you got there," Dicky said.

"Where's your Hawaiian shirt?" Ross asked, quickly looking over his shoulder. "It's a luau."

"I don't need one. Nobody cares."

That's when it hit Ross. Dicky was about the same size as Ross. Same hair color. Similar build. Craig was blind with his glasses. It was dark out back.

"Where's your spirit?" Ross unbuttoned his shirt. "I'll trade you."

"Really?"

"I was leaving soon anyway," Ross said. "That was a thing. People making fun of your clothes when we were kids. So mean. This way you can fit in."

"Actually," Dicky started to say.

"Let's swap."

They traded shirts. Ross was dancing a little in anticipation of Craig's inevitable arrival.

"Do you got to piss or something?" Dicky asked.

Very loud crashing and screaming rose from the bar. Ross and Dicky turned at the same time.

"Yeah, I do." Ross walked quickly to the corner, as deep into the shadows as he could.

The backdoor flew open. Craig Morgan stepped outside. He saw Dicky Dirt right away, standing in the middle of the closed area.

"You're a dead man," Craig shouted.

"Why?" was all Dicky was able to get out.

To say that Dicky Dirt took a beating would not do justice to the extent of his dismantling. When it was all over, his body lay twisted and writhing on the ground. His breathing sounded raspy and damaged. Small moans followed even the smallest movement. It looked like he had been dunked in a vat of beet juice. Whatever wasn't bloody was bruised. One of his shoes had come off.

When Craig eventually walked back into the bar, he left Dicky Dirt on the damp, stinking ground. The sewage seeped up from the ground and soaked Dicky's clothes from the bottom up. A beating was one thing, but nobody deserved an infection.

Ross laid out a couple beach towels before he helped Dicky Dirt onto his sofa. The couch was old, ragged, and babyshit green, but that didn't mean he wanted blood all over it.

It hadn't mattered. The moment Ross set him down, Dicky vomited all over himself, Ross, and about a third of the living room.

"Sorry," Dicky said through his busted mouth.

Ross wiped the puke off his face and walked into the kitchen. He dry-heaved once but kept it down. It wasn't the first time someone vomited on his face. At least this time it wasn't during sex. He rinsed off in the sink and grabbed another towel.

Dicky Dirt was a mess. His nose was broken. The swelling on one eye looked like someone adhered a plum to his face and then stepped on it. His lips were double-sized and split in places. There was a lump on his forehead that was damn near an antler. Under his clothes, Dicky was most certainly purple with bruises.

Ross couldn't help but feel partly responsible for Dicky's condition. It made him feel weird inside. Regret or guilt or empathy, he didn't know which, as those were words he had seen and knew the meaning of, but had never bothered to experience.

"What happened?" Dicky said. Or at least, that's what

Ross assumed he said. It was mostly spitty, juicy sounds in the shape of "What happened?"

"I don't know," Ross said. "Craig Morgan lost his shit. He went berserker on you. Did you do something to piss him off?"

Dicky shook his head, but froze when he cringed at the pain. He shrugged, but that looked like it hurt too.

"You must have done something," Ross said.

"Where am I?"

"You're at my place. Boog didn't want cops or an ambulance showing up again. Wanted to keep his current streak going. Six days might be a new record."

"Can't afford anyway."

"Who can? You can stay here for a bit. If you're pissing blood after two days—'cause you'll definitely be pissing blood today—then you should probably get to the doctor. Internal injuries don't always fix themselves."

"Thanks, Ross."

"Anything for Dicky Dirt."

Dicky stared at him. Ross took the look in his eye to be gratitude for his kindness. Ross started to feel better about things. None of that guilt or whatever. He was kind of a hero, if he thought about it.

Dicky had gotten so much hell in high school. Bullied by everyone. A pizza-faced geek with a huge Adam's apple, but his real sin was that his family was dirt poor. It wasn't like the small desert town had debutante balls, but there was still a social strata between the poor and the really poor. He was an untouchable.

He never had new clothes, always decades-old hand-me-downs. And those clothes were never clean. That's how he got his name. Ross doubted that he had running water inside the trailer and probably used the camp facilities.

Ross could remember at least three times when Dicky Dirt got the stuffing beat out of him for no reason other than existing. People chanting his name while someone used him as a punching bag.

The least Ross could do was help out the poor guy.

Two days later, Dicky said he felt better. The swelling had gone down on both his eyes and his lip. The purple had become a rainbow of yellows and greens. He could talk better, although he still drooled out of one corner of his mouth.

"I'll be out of your hair soon," Dicky said. "Just got to find a place to stay."

"Don't you got a place?"

"Not no more. Long story. Roommate disagreement. Kicked me out the night I saw you. I was fixing on sleeping in some patch of the desert. Getting drunk enough to put up with the coyotes and scorps. Then Craig showed up."

"Sucks."

"Terry wouldn't even let me take my stuff."

Ross started to worry that Dicky Dirt would never leave. It was one thing to help a guy who just got his ass handed to him, but he didn't want this gross dude fusing to his couch. He'd already ruined his good towel.

"My sister said she knew a guy that had a room. I'm going to call him."

Ross felt some relief, but wanted a sure thing.

"Won't do much good," Dicky said, "unless I can get my stuff. My money is with my stuff."

"I can go by and get it."

"It's trickier than that. My old roommate is a dick of historic proportions. Terry wouldn't give just hand you my stuff. I'll have to get my money some other way. Maybe borrow a gun."

"How much money are you talking about?" Ross said.

"Don't know. Whatever I made in the last month selling weed. A couple grand. I don't really count it until I need to."

Ross never ignored an opportunity. He could definitely

skim some off the top or better yet, tell Dicky that there was no money. Dicky would still have his clothes and toothbrush. Everyone would win.

"What's the address?" Ross said. "I can break in when this dude Terry is out."

"You would do that?" Dicky smiled. It made the corners of his mouth bleed. "I'll pay you like a commission or a finder's fee. Ten percent sound fair?

"Absolutely." Ross gave him a pat on the shoulder. "More than fair."

Dicky winced.

The house was the same as the others on the block, a stucco job with a terra cotta tile roof. The backyard fence was wood, not chain link, which meant that if Ross got back there, he could operate unseen from the street.

Ross parked just around the corner. Dicky fidgeted in the passenger seat trying to get comfortable.

"Terry's car is in the driveway, but he'll take off in the next hour. He always gets his dinner at that taco place where the Naugles used to be. The one off the freeway."

"It's been like twenty different things since the Naugles closed. Location is cursed."

"No point in remembering the name."

"What's that? About eight, ten miles away?"

"Something like that. It'll give you a half hour and change."

"Should be plenty," Ross said. He was getting excited. He hadn't broken into a house since he was a teenager. And that hadn't been to steal, but to watch people sleep. He was not proud of that creepy chapter in his life, but teenagers were morons, so also not unexpected.

"There's a key in a fake rock near the back door. If it's not there, you'll need to bust a window. There's no alarm though."

"What all am I getting?"

"When you get inside, you'll be in the kitchen. Go straight. There will be a hall to your right. Second door on the left. Two big duffel bags on the top shelf of the closet. Shouldn't be heavy."

"Do I got to worry about neighbors? Anyone going to call the cops?"

"It ain't that kind of neighborhood."

They stared straight ahead at the Ford F-150 in the driveway.

"Why did you give me your shirt at Boog's?" Dicky asked.

"Hunh?" Ross turned to him. "I don't know. I was leaving. It was a luau. I didn't want you to look like a dick. Remembered all the shit you got in high school."

"You were thinking of when we were kids?"

Ross shrugged, but movement in the driveway caught his attention.

The guy that walked out of the front door did not look like a Terry. He looked like a guy with a nickname. The Beast or Skullcrusher, if you were going right at it. Tiny or Peewee, if you were being ironic. A big Mexican dude in a wife beater, tattoo sleeves down both arms and trapezius muscles that connected his ears to his shoulders. Ross wasn't convinced that the gargantuan could turn his head.

"That's Terry?"

"That's why I can't just walk in and get my stuff."

"He looks like a criminal. Or a monster. He looks like a monster criminal."

"He's a florist."

"That guy arranges flowers for a living?"

"If you're scared," Dicky said, "you don't have to do this."

Of course Ross was scared, but he wasn't about to let Dicky Dirt know that. He was the alpha in this equation.

He would use that fear. It was the adrenaline boost that he

needed. He could still remember the buzz when he perved out as a teenager. The anticipation of breaking into someone else's home was exhilarating. He had been a creepy little bastard.

Crossing the street in a crouch, he looked back at Dicky who gave him a smile and a thumbs-up.

Ross gave the street a quick look to the left and right. Clear. He climbed the wooden fence. Climb was generous. He lifted himself up to about half a chin-up, tried to swing up his leg, failed, started to pendulum back and forth until he finally hooked his ankle on the top of the fence. He stayed frozen in that position for a moment, not sure what was next. He wiggled his foot until it was over the fence more and eventually straddled it, splinters digging through his jeans into his balls. He hopped off the top and landed on his knees in the backyard. They didn't make a comforting sound.

Dicky hadn't said anything about a dog.

To be fair, Corgis weren't traditional guard dogs, so maybe Dicky didn't think the creature warranted a mention. A German Shepherd or a Rottweiler, sure, that would have come up. Adorably goofy didn't mean that the damn thing didn't have teeth.

Ross laughed at first as the tube of dog ran at him on its stubby legs. It stopped being funny when it grabbed his pant leg and pulled. The dog nicked his ankle with surprisingly sharp teeth. He kicked at it, but it was alarmingly agile for an animal with no knees.

"Screw it." Ross stood up, pretending like the dog wasn't there. He walked to the backdoor with the tenacious beast attached to his leg.

The bowl next to the door said "Lucky." Ever the optimist, Ross took it as a good sign that the animal trying to sever his ankle arteries was his good luck charm.

That optimism lasted up until Lucky bit his hand when he lifted a rock to look for the key. The backyard was almost entirely rocks and every time he reached for one, Lucky snapped at him.

"That's it," Ross said, pointing at the dog. "Me and you, we got a problem."

Ross picked up the dog. It squirmed in his arms and snapped at him. His first instinct was to throw it over the fence or onto the roof, but he didn't believe in hurting animals. Except for geese, but they suck.

He looked around the backyard. There was a weight bench and a doghouse. That would do. He grabbed a twenty-five-pound plate with one hand, still holding the growling dog in the other. Ross chucked the dog into the doghouse and blocked the door with the plate, digging it into the ground, but making sure there was a small opening at the top so the dog could breathe.

He didn't bother with finding the key. Ross chucked a twenty-pound dumbbell through the backdoor window and reached inside to unlock the door.

The kitchen was a kitchen. Who gives a shit about kitchens. He stubbed his toe and tripped on the dumbbell that he had thrown through the window. When he put his hand to the ground to catch his balance, he caught some broken glass.

"Damn it."

His hand bled in a pour. He grabbed the dish towel that hung from the refrigerator door and quickly wrapped his hand. The towel smelled like parmesan cheese and dry salami. It immediately became saturated with blood.

Leaving a drip down the hallway, Ross walked to the second door on the left. It opened into a bedroom furnished with a mattress, a massive TV, and a game console of some kind. Ross had never gotten into gaming. He had gotten the Tempest high score at the 7-Eleven when he was fifteen and decided to retire on top. He never looked back.

It was pretty much how he pictured Dicky Dirt's bedroom.

The guy was such a loser. He didn't know if he should take the console too, but Dicky had only said the two duffels. If there was room, he would throw it inside.

The closet door was locked, which Ross found strange. The closet doors at his place didn't have locks. It would have been easier if Dicky had told him about it and given him a key, but there were a lot of ways to open a locked door.

Ross walked back to the kitchen, picked up the dumbbell, cut himself again, swore all the swears that he knew, and returned to the bedroom.

It took about a dozen sharp blows, one bruised thumb, and a torn-off fingernail, but he managed to get the door open.

There were clothes in the closet, but that wasn't what caught his eye. The duffel bags were on the top shelf. But again, not what he was focused on. He was far more interested in the firearms. All of them. Three assault rifles and three shotguns sat propped against the back wall.

He grabbed the duffels from the shelf. One heavy, one lighter.

Dicky had not been straight with him, that's for sure. Something strange was going on. Ross had felt a little bad that he was going to steal the guy's money, but now he wasn't so sure that Dicky didn't need to be robbed.

Ross opened the first bag. It was packed with weed. The second bag was full of money. Like a lot of money. More than two grand. Too much money.

Weed, money, guns.

That's when he heard the front door close.

Ross spun around in a circle, looking for a hiding place that wasn't there. He considered diving under the mattress. If he made his body really flat, it could work. Except that his body couldn't do flat. It was too round in the center.

He attempted to open the window, but it was painted shut.

He heard footsteps coming closer. He lifted again, feeling a sharp pain running from his shoulder into his lower back. He managed to get the window open enough to squeeze through. Then he saw the metal bars. It really wasn't his day.

He ran into the closet, closing the door behind him all but a crack. He waited and listened. Footsteps. A door. Some grunting and swearing. A flushing toilet.

The bedroom door opened. Ross watched Terry pass through the sliver of light from the door. He sunk back further into the closet. He heard Terry plop onto the mattress, relieved that he had aborted the mattress plan.

Ross only saw two options. He could wait it out. Or he could grab the shotgun sitting next to him and kamikaze it. He knew which was the more manly choice.

He decided to wait it out. He could be a man later. Men could be reasonable and slightly cowardly and still be men.

A half hour later, Terry was snoring and Ross saw his chance. He texted Dicky that he would be coming out the front door fast. He put a duffel bag on each arm and grabbed the shotgun.

Ross pushed open the closet door. It creaked loudly. Ross stopped and waited. Nothing. He pushed it a little more. Same thing. Ross paused again. He poked his head around the edge of the doorway. Terry was immobile.

Ross counted to three, and then rushed to the door. Unfortunately he held the shotgun across his body. It hit the door jamb and slammed against his belly. He oofed, but that wasn't the noise that woke up Terry. It was the shotgun blast from accidentally pulling the trigger.

"Of course," Ross said. He dropped the shotgun and ran for the front door, a duffel bag draped over each shoulder.

He didn't know what Terry said behind him. It was more of a roar. It definitely wasn't a friendly greeting.

***

The moment Ross stepped out the front door, he was greeted with a fist. It felt like someone squashed a tomato against his face, but that had been his nose. He dropped to the porch and looked up at Dicky Dirt who smiled back at him, busted lip and missing tooth and all.

"What the hell, Dicky Dirt?" Ross said.

Terry appeared in the doorway above him, growling. The two men looked down at Ross and the duffel bags.

"Hey, Punishment," Dicky said. "I saw this guy running out of your house."

Ross didn't know what was happening, but Punishment definitely fit the man better than Terry. Even in the present circumstance, he could acknowledge a badass sobriquet.

"Thanks," Punishment said to Dicky. "What's your name again?"

"Richard. I buy weed from you now and again. Deal a little. We played some Madden a few months ago."

"I remember. You kicked my ass."

Dicky laughed. "I was passing by. Saw this loser."

"I owe you, man."

"Dicky Dirt set me up," Ross said, but knew that sounded stupid.

"Don't rough the guy up too much," Dicky said. "Probably a desperate junkie."

"Watch him for a second." Punishment grabbed the duffel bags and walked back in the house. Ross thought he heard him say to himself, "Where did I put those tin snips?"

Ross tried to stand, but Dicky kicked his arm, knocking him back down.

"If you run," Dicky said, "Punishment will make it worse."

"What the hell, Dicky?"

"I saw an opportunity and I took it. A chance for revenge."

"What did I ever do to you?"

"Come on. You know."

"All of this because I tricked Craig Morgan into kicking

the shit out of you? I didn't know he was going to pummel you so hard."

"Not that. You gave me the name Dicky Dirt. I came to school one day and was wearing—wait a minute. What did you just say? Oh, hell no. That shit with Craig was your fault? Now I don't feel bad at all about what Punishment is going to do. You're still a dick. This was about the past. You making up that damn name. Everyone calling me Dicky Dirt from then on out."

"Did I?" Ross asked. "I don't even remember doing that."

Punishment returned. He grabbed Ross by the back of the shirt and dragged him into the house. The last thing Ross saw before Punishment kicked the door shut was Dicky Dirt licking his finger, trying to get some of Ross's blood off his shirt.

MR. KIPPER
Inspired by the Rhyming Slang for Jack the Ripper
Paul Finch

Pamela supposed she ought to be happy that a man was coming to work with her. Okay, she wouldn't know him, and it would be an awkward first couple of days but at least it would afford her an extra degree of security. That was what she hoped. If he turned out to be an oddball, she didn't think she'd be able to cope, but even in her most anxiety-filled moments, she couldn't picture a loutish type wanting to take up a post at *Book-a-Thon*.

Apart from anything else, it was completely unpaid. The only thing you got here was coffee, assuming you remembered to pick some up yourself when the tin ran out. On top of that, the hours were quite long—it was open nine-till-five Monday to Friday, but also on Saturdays from ten in the morning until three in the afternoon. In addition, the work was boring. All you did most of the day was stand behind the front counter, say hello to people when they came in, collect their contributions, keep half an eye on them as they browsed the shelves looking to take something away in return, and then insert the new acquisitions into the appropriate gaps after they'd gone.

Pamela just couldn't see some hooligan or degenerate wanting a deal like that.

In any case, in reflection of most of their customers, this new chap would likely be somewhere between middle-aged and old. She sipped her coffee and glanced at her watch. It was just after 1:30 p.m. on a Tuesday, and there were only three people present: herself and Mrs. Brody, who was busying herself in their small kitchen, and their sole customer of the day, old Mr. Banks.

It wasn't as if they could fit lots of people in anyway.

Five yards in front of the counter was the glass front door. To the right, an internal door stood open on what they called 'the Library'. It wasn't a real library; just a room about the size of a classroom, its walls lined with shelves, its central area divided up into avenues by long, library-type bookcases. Despite that, they had near enough everything in there, from thrillers to romance, from horror to history. In those terms it was near enough the equivalent of a library—they'd done very well considering that everything was donated.

Even so, at present a single person was availing himself of it: Mr. Banks, who only came in to read the newspapers. A small coffee table sat in the centre of the Library, with three armchairs around it. Mr. Banks occupied the one facing away. Those dailies he'd already read lay discarded on the table, and he was now buried in a broadsheet. This was his usual ritual. He'd come in here just before noon and would be out again at around two. Though Heaven knew, there was enough in the papers today, even the local rag, an ad-filled freesheet called the *Brookshaw Courier*, to keep a hundred readers glued to their pages for the rest of the day.

Its headline that morning read: *NUMBER FOUR!*

The story told how the body of a young woman found two days ago half-submerged in the filthy waters of the Leeds/Liverpool Canal, shredded beyond recognition, was thought to be Sarah Galloway, a Manchester University student who'd disappeared on her way home from college. Under pressure, a police spokesman had now admitted the strong possibility that she was the fourth victim of an unknown assailant who'd already struck three times since the previous June. The first two had been sex workers, but the third had been a nurse coming off shift, and now there was this one. All four of them had been found stabbed and mutilated in isolated spots across Greater Manchester.

Pamela felt uncomfortably at her ribs, which seemed to ache as she probed them. That was psychosomatic, Gerald had told her; it was perfectly natural and nothing to worry about. Dr. Atkins had agreed, but when the news broke that the third victim had been found on wasteland just outside Brookshaw, he'd been sufficiently concerned by Pamela's hurriedly-made appointment and hugely elevated stress levels to increase her dosage of Prozac.

Gerald had been less conciliatory.

'Darling…it's awful, I agree. Unspeakably tragic. A life's been lost, but you really can't be taking this sort of thing personally. Like the doctor said, be logical. There are crimes and murders every day. But this is not a conspiracy against *you*.'

'Gerald…he's getting closer each time. The first one was in central Manchester, the second one a bit nearer, the one after that on the outskirts of Brookshaw itself…'

'Pamela, whoever *he* is, he'll go wherever the hunting takes him…'

'And he's not just targeting prostitutes anymore.'

'He probably never was. All these poor women will be targets of convenience. But that still doesn't mean that this is about *you*.'

'I know it's not about me, but what if…'

'Just give it a rest, yeah? I can't take it, darling! I've bloody had enough!'

He'd been so vexed after that that she'd barely said anything when the fourth victim, the student, was found in the canal not two miles from where she now stood. Such proximity, however, had perhaps been a little too close even for Gerald's liking. On first hearing the story, he'd raised the subject himself.

'It's still not about *you*, darling.' He'd used a softer tone that morning, almost kind. 'There's a madman on the loose... there's no denying it. But the police are everywhere. They're saying there's a hundred detectives working on the case.'

'Have they given him a name yet?' she'd asked in a small voice. She could have found that out by reading the newspaper articles for herself, but instead she averted her eyes whenever she caught sight of one. She even turned the television off when the news came on.

'I wouldn't know,' he'd replied disapprovingly. 'I haven't looked past the basic details. It's all salacious silliness, anyway.'

Which translates into 'he has, but it's too horrible to tell you about.'

'Thank you, Mrs. Patterson.'

Pamela almost jumped out of her skin.

'Bad business,' Mr. Banks said, offering the newspapers in a dog-eared bundle. She nodded and agreed that it was, surreptitiously turning the papers upside down before pushing them to the corner of the counter.

'Four victims in as many months,' he added with doleful relish.

'That's what I hear, yes,' she said, praying that the old man would go away.

He fastened his overcoat, his long, pale, grey-veined hands fumbling with each button. Briefly, Pamela found her attention fixed on those ugly hands. She thought about Thomas Hallam again, and had to clench her teeth.

'Cold out,' he commented pulling on a pair of woolly gloves.

'Yes, it is. Late October, after all.'

'Aye. Nights are drawing in.'

Thanks for the reminder.

Pamela had first started volunteering here back in May, Gerald and Dr. Atkins having finally persuaded her that if she didn't get out and about, even if it wasn't getting back to full-time work yet, her fears would transpose into full-blown agoraphobia and she'd end up a prisoner in her own home. And Thomas Hallam would have won.

But it had been early summer then. Warm, bright days. Young mothers in sandals and dresses pushing prams. The on/off jingle of ice cream vans. How that relaxed atmosphere had diminished with the onset of damper, cooler air, with the shriveling and falling of leaves, with the shorter afternoons and longer, darker evenings.

Today was October 27, and even though the hour didn't go back until tomorrow, sunset now arrived at 5:30 p.m. This meant that by the time she finished here, it was already dark. Thankfully, Gerald had agreed to pick her up in the evenings, though it was an inconvenience for him, as it meant he'd have to leave the office earlier than he liked.

And doesn't he show it.

But this had been part of the deal when she'd agreed to rejoin the rat-race. She wouldn't have to walk home again, or even catch the bus until she felt she was ready for it.

'You all right, Mrs. Patterson?'

'What…oh yes, fine.' She forced a smile.

Mr. Banks had finished with his overcoat and gloves. 'Just mind how you go…when you're on your way home tonight, yes?'

'I'm sorry?'

In retrospect, it was an obvious thing for him to have said. They'd been talking about the murders and had mentioned that it had been getting darker earlier. Why wouldn't he move swiftly on to the next obvious subject, which was the danger this posed?

'I'm getting a lift,' she said hurriedly.

He nodded at that and left her with a contemplative half-smile, as if for some reason this information didn't entirely please him.

Whoa, hang on! You don't suppose...?

Just as quickly, Pamela dismissed the notion. She'd misconstrued things that was all. He hadn't looked disappointed that she'd be riding home in her husband's car but had merely been taking the matter seriously. She ought to be touched that he was concerned for her. If nothing else, Banks was easily into his eighties, and this maniac had apparently been cutting his victims to pieces. What kind of strength and aggression would that require?

Be super-ironic if the madman had been in here with you all along, wouldn't it?

Pamela shook her head, trying to shake the idea free.

There was no danger *here*. There were never less than two members of staff on duty. And even though Mrs. Brody was going on leave tomorrow, there'd be another one coming in.

The man.

Yeah...great.

'All well, dear?' Mrs. Brody enquired, coming out from the kitchen.

She was a short, tubby woman of about forty, with stiff red hair and stern features, whose squat figure now that she was six months pregnant looked positively rotund.

'Fine. Just been chatting to Mr. Banks.'

Mrs. Brody pulled an irritated face. 'Another one who contributes nothing to the operation.'

Ever since she'd been here, Pamela had thought Mrs. Brody a tad shrewish in attitude given that most of their customers couldn't afford to buy new books. One Scottish chap, called Ogilvy, was slightly different. He regularly brought in cartons crammed with books of his own, which he wanted to donate, and never took more than a handful in return. However, on the last occasion, Mrs. Brody had stopped him on his way out, because he'd taken five paperbacks in exchange for two box-loads which had to contain at least a hundred.

'Excuse me,' she'd said. 'The rule is that you take three,

and no more.'

He'd gazed at her with an expression implicit with all the disdain the common man felt for the jobsworths of Britain, before trudging back into the Library, and replacing two books on the shelves.

'It seems harsh,' Mrs. Brody had commented later. 'But we can't have people helping themselves. There'll be nothing left.'

Pamela hadn't bothered replying that a valuable and generous source of free books was now unlikely to darken their doors again. She only wanted a quiet life while she was here, which was never easy with such an overbearing personality in the role of self-appointed manager. In many ways it was a relief that Mrs. Brody would shortly be going on leave. Pamela just hoped that this new staff member, the man, would have no, well…

Let's not pussyfoot around it. If he's a weirdo, you're leaving too.

Yes. And wouldn't Gerald be happy then.

As it was her last day, Mrs. Brody left earlier than she usually would, just after 3:30 p.m. It was a disagreeable surprise for Pamela, as it meant she'd be manning the operation alone for the next two hours. Mrs. Brody, who clearly hadn't thought about this, even though she knew about Pamela's past, made the helpful suggestion that Pamela leave early too.

Yeah, that'll work. Get Gerald out of the office mid-afternoon, to run you home. He'll be well-pleased.

So, she stayed behind on her own. There wasn't any other option.

As soon as Mrs. Brody had gone, she locked the front door, turned the lights off behind the counter, and moved through into the Library, where she drew the curtains and left only one light on so that no one would realize she was in here.

After that, she sat in the armchair where Mr. Banks had

studied the newspapers, furious at her own cowardice.

Except that maybe it wasn't quite like that.

'One step at a time,' Dr. Atkins had told her. 'You've been through a ghastly ordeal. It isn't easy returning to normal life after something like that. And stop listening to these voices in your head, these primal fears which the whole business has awakened. Apply logic, instead.'

I wonder if Sarah Galloway was a student of logic?

'No...no.' Pamela shook her head to clear her mind. It wasn't silly, locking herself away like this. Not when all she wanted was a breather. Not when she was trying to get over a breakdown. Even people who'd been mildly ill were owed some recuperation time.

Standing up, she opted to pass the next hour and a half by reading a good book.

It still wasn't dark outside, but the gloom of the autumn evening was fast descending. It was even gloomier inside, of course, with all the curtains drawn.

Okay, open them again. Let him know you're on your own.

Without the single light, she wouldn't even have been able to read the titles on the book spines. Though that particular light, as it happened, was located just above the *Thrillers* section. With a dull sense of foreboding, Pamela grabbed down the first three she saw.

Oh yes, excellent choices here...

Titles like *These I Kill*, *Slaughter in the Dark* and *I, Madman* trapped the breath in her throat. While their various covers—a hooded figure hunched against a desolate cityscape, a clown mask with blood trailing from either corner of its mouth, and a woman's sweating, terrified face, bruised eyes bulging—almost had her knees buckling.

If that wasn't enough, Pamela then heard a loud rustling of paper.

She stiffened, the paperbacks dropping from her hands,

clattering loudly on the polished tiled floor. Now, there were only muffled traffic sounds from beyond the curtains.

But then she heard it again.

A rustling, scrunching noise. Paper, cardboard, or both.

She pivoted slowly, squinting into the furthest recesses of the Library. It wasn't so dim that she couldn't make out the free-standing bookcases, but of course there were spaces been them into which she couldn't see.

She was resolute that she'd keep her nerve. It wasn't possible for someone to have entered except through the front door, where she'd have spotted them easily.

Aren't you forgetting the fire-door?

That was in the far corner, screened from where Pamela currently stood. She wondered if Mrs. Brody might have left it open for some reason, though that would have been ridiculously unlike her. Heart thudding, she headed over that way, circling around *History*, venturing down the aisle between *Romance* and *Science Fiction*. This brought her to an intersection, from where, if she looked right, she would see the fire-door in question. It would still be closed; she was sure.

Yeah?

She took a chance and peeked.

It *was* closed.

Emboldened, she advanced, pressing it with her fingertips. It was closed properly.

Feeling worse than foolish, Pamela trekked back into the centre of the Library, but continued to listen. Was it possible she'd heard a bird against one of the windows?

Yeah, because that happens all the time.

Baffled, she went back to the counter. Beyond the glass door, the day was turning into dusk, but she could still see everything. The paved path, which was littered with red and gold leaves, ran straight as a die for ten yards, emerging through a gateless gap in a wrought-iron fence onto Widdrington Lane. Even as she looked, cars rumbled past. An old woman went by with shopping bag.

Normality. Life going on as usual.

Pamela cringed inwardly, again torn by loathing of her own frailty.

How could this have happened? That someone like her—a highly-paid legal secretary attached to a famous old law firm, glamorous wife to a successful businessman, hostess of a dozen high-class dinner parties—could be reduced to the status of nervous recluse?

Another sound intruded: again, the crackle of paper.

Pamela spun around, staring bug-eyed into the mouth of the staff-only corridor behind the counter. There couldn't be anyone down there. That corridor connected with only three rooms: the kitchen, the toilet and the Stock Room at the back, as they called it…

So, that noise made itself?

Pamela's hand slid again to the phone in her jeans pocket. Surely the police would come immediately if she called, the last murder having happened only two miles from here? But what if there was some embarrassingly mundane explanation? She wouldn't just look a prize fool, but a neurotic idiot.

One step at a time, the doctor had said.

But that only worked if you occasionally took those steps.

Clutching the phone like a weapon, she lifted the counter hatch and stepped through into the staff area.

More paper crackled.

A rat maybe? Bridgewater House wasn't an especially old building, but it was cheaply thrown together; a single-story affair from the '60s or '70s, originally a children's primary school and later a kind of community centre. *Book-a-Thon* was only one section of it.

Encouraged by the thought, though at one time she'd have been appalled, she moved into the corridor entrance. She reached for the light switch, but again hesitated.

Since getting married ten years ago, she and Gerald had lived in Fairvale, Brookshaw's swishest suburb. Constantly fearing burglary, they'd taken many precautions. A police advisor had told them that if they ever heard anyone breaking in at night, the best thing to do was lock themselves in their bedroom, turning lights on to alert the interlopers and frighten them away. But this was the specified course of action when an intruder was on your property to steal, rather than…

Gut you like a fish? Hack your arms and legs off?

More paperwork rattled from the shadowy corridor.

Pamela's hand remained fast on the light switch, but she didn't activate it. On this occasion, it was almost certainly better that whoever it was—if it was anyone at all—was *not* informed that they'd been discovered.

Stiff as iron, she ventured down the passage. When she reached the kitchen, she glanced breathlessly in. The fading light outside penetrated the high, frosted window just sufficiently to show that there was nobody in there. A similarly reduced light spilled from the next two open doorways. When she glanced into the toilet, that was also unoccupied, which left only the Stock Room.

Pamela paused before the final door, the breath struggling in her constricted chest.

'Go on, darling,' Gerald would have said. 'Face your demons.'

'Be logical,' Dr. Atkins had told her.

Logic dictating that, as this lunatic butchers women for fun, you should be going the other way!

Sweat dabbling her forehead, Pamela pushed forward through the open door.

The evening dimness was intensifying, but she could see that clearly that there was no one else here. To ensure there was no mistake, she hit the light-switch. The small room was indeed empty, aside from a table, a stool and a couple of boxes of donated books too tatty to put on the shelves. Even as she stood there, there was another crackle of paper, but this time Pamela traced it to the high letterbox window in the corner, the frosted pane of which hung open. She pulled the stool over, climbed up and peered out into the drab, open-air quadrangle located at the centre of Bridgewater House. Directly across from her, perhaps twenty yards away, one of the women who worked in the Mothers & Babies Club, where they'd had a birthday party that afternoon, was cramming wrapping paper into a wheelie-bin.

Sagging with embarrassed relief, Pamela tried to close the window, but it wouldn't fasten, its rusted metal catch snapping when she tried to force it.

Better that than your neck.

She slumped down onto the stool, unable to believe how much sweat came from her forehead when she wiped it with her fingers.

As she headed back down the staff corridor, she wondered how many pointless scares like this she would need to endure before she started to get well. How many times she would have to prove to herself that everything was okay.

She walked out behind the counter, glancing through the glass door again.

And there was a man on the path, gazing in.

Instinctively, she jumped backwards into the corridor.

You really think he didn't see you?

After the surging relief of the last few seconds, Pamela was stiff with fear all over again. She hadn't seen much of him, the merest glimpse, but some things had registered. He'd been young, tall, broad at the shoulder, wearing denims. A good ten seconds passed as she waited there, not just shocked but confused, trying to work out what this might signify.

Three heavy knocks sounded on the glass, reverberating through the whole building.

Pamela's breathing was now so shallow that she barely felt it.

A moment, and then three more knocks sounded.

There was obviously no point hiding. He'd seen her, and

he wasn't going to go away.

Another three knocks. Very loud and impatient this time.

'Alright!' she yelped, stepping out behind the counter.

He was close on the other side, peering through the glass with cupped hands. A young man, somewhere in his early twenties, wearing jeans and a denim jacket over an old T-shirt. He had unruly, collar-length hair, and a thick moustache. He carried what looked like a rucksack over his left shoulder and held a smaller cloth bag in his right hand.

'Excuse me, missus,' he said. 'Are you open? It's just that the sign says you are.'

Damning herself for a fool, Pamela realized that, when she'd locked up earlier, she'd neglected to turn the 'Open' sign around.

'Erm…I'm not, no,' she replied. 'We've had to close early.'

'Oh…right.'

He didn't seem like an unpleasant man, she thought. In fact, he looked a little dropped on.

'It's just…well, I go to the Tech,' he said, referencing the A-Level College not three streets away. 'I usually get picked up by my dad at the end of the road here…you know, when he's coming home from work. I've seen you open a few times, and I wondered if you might be interested in these old textbooks?'

He held up the cloth bag.

That would be a nice gesture, Pamela realized. Students at the Tech usually sold their old textbooks. But she would still need to open the door to take them off him.

'It's very kind of you,' she said, stalling. 'But I'd need to go and find the keys, and that might, erm…it might take…'

A pair of headlights pulled up beyond the gate. Pamela spied the dented, green bodywork of what looked like an old transit van. The young man glanced around.

'My old fella's here,' he said. 'That means I've got to go. Tell you what…' He placed the books on the step and edged backwards. 'They'll be okay here, wont they...while you go looking for the key? It's not raining, or nothing.'

'Okay...right. That's an excellent idea. Thanks.'

She had to shout because his back was already turned as he hurried away, jumping into the front passenger seat of the vehicle, which pulled off away.

Pamela's head drooped as she pondered the ludicrousness of the situation, tears mingling with the sweat on her cheeks. Eventually, she went out through the hatch and unlocked the glass door.

You've seen the bushes down either side of the path? Someone could be hiding.

Reminding herself that the bushes were largely leafless, she stepped determinedly outside, reclaimed the bag from the step, and taking it back indoors, examined the contents.

Three textbooks, as promised. *The Enlightenment*, *The Rise of National Thought* and *The Early Modern Age*. Good, solid hardbacks, in excellent condition—they almost looked new.

And Pamela had nearly turned them away.

She sighed as she re-bagged them and left them on the counter. She'd find space for them on the shelves tomorrow. In the meantime, she needed to get fixed up. Gerald would be here soon, and he wouldn't be impressed to see that she'd been crying.

A few minutes later, after touching up the minimal make-up she wore these days, she grabbed her mac and bag, hit the lights and locked up behind her. Gerald's Mercedes was waiting at the end of the path. She walked quickly towards it, glancing neither right nor left.

It was too easy to imagine that someone could be crouching in those bushes. But at least Gerald was here now.

It won't be a problem tomorrow either...because then you'll have the man.

* * *

He was well enough presented, in a superficial sort of way, wearing an Italian leather jacket, a short-sleeved shirt with a neck chain showing, pressed trousers and polished brogues. He had handsome, chiseled features, with short, dark hair slicked to one side. But there was an air of cunning about him. He seemed relaxed and confident as he sat in the office chair, unusually so given the reason he was here.

When Pamela asked if he'd like coffee, he shook his head. Even before she'd sat back at her own desk, he'd lost interest in her, muttering to himself, cracking his knuckles. This drew her attention to his hands, which looked disproportionately large, knobbled and hairy, a single, black star tattooed on the back of the left one. When his gaze suddenly darted back towards her, she averted her eyes, but felt pinned in place as he silently and protractedly appraised her. He was looking at her legs, she realized. That wasn't unusual. There was no modesty board, and at Gerald's urging she'd always adopted the 'office glam' approach: high heels, pencil skirt, silk blouse, blond hair cut in a fetching bob.

'Always make the best of yourself, darling,' as her hubby had once said. 'Don't listen to that feminist claptrap. Sure, you want the bosses to value you for your efficiency. But all legal secretaries are efficient. You've got *extra* tools—use them.'

At that moment, her 'tools' felt as if they might be a disadvantage.

Thomas Hallam was here to see his solicitors, because he was under suspicion of two rapes. He'd already been arrested and bailed once, but as the police collected more evidence, it was increasingly likely that he'd be arrested again—and now he was feasting his eyes on *her*. At least, she *thought* he was, because she wouldn't dare look up and meet his gaze.

Not that she had much choice several hours later, when crossing the underground car park and he sprang out from behind a concrete stanchion.

It was weird how the first thing to go through Pamela's mind was fascination that he'd been prepared to wait most of the day for her, though further consideration was scrambled as he hit her on the side of the head with pile-driving force. All thoughts went tumbling, the next blow coming from the asphalt floor as she hit it full-length. Before she knew it, one of those big, knobbly paws had twisted into her hair, and he was lugging her away through the oil and grime. The far end of this parking level was undergoing renovation. There were cones down there, and strips of tape. And beyond those, a wall of black shadow.

'Bitch is going to pay,' he chuckled to himself. 'Oh yes. Pay up, totty bitch.'

And then the lift doors opened again, and more male voices intruded, penetrating Pamela's stupor. They were engaged in cheery banter, though this rapidly stuttered to a halt. Then there was a chaos of angry shouting.

Pamela's head hit the floor again as her hair was released. His face swam down to hers, his eyes moon-like, his mouth fizzing with fetid saliva.

'Upper class tart,' he hissed. 'You haven't got away…you hear?'

A bomb exploded in her stomach, and his feet slammed her side with rib-cracking impacts.

Though her physical scars had long faded, every time Pamela relived the experience in her dreams, the pain was just as intense. At least fleetingly.

On this occasion, though it was still three in the morning, she hobbled weakly downstairs. In the kitchen, she sat on a stool, shivering, while the kettle boiled. Her usual routine was to make herself coffee. It was hardly ideal in the middle of the might, but then sleep was often an ordeal in itself.

In truth, she could have cried, but one of the few things Gerald said about this that *did* ring true was that self-pity only isolated a person more, and that you at least had to make an effort to be strong, otherwise you'd end up with no allies at all. Of course, he'd then ruined the whole thing by extending the argument to her new choice of haircut, which was very short—'mannish', in his words—and her unconscious renunciation of the pretty, designer clothes she'd once worn religiously. 'Trading your Gucci handbag in for a piece of cloth with a shoulder-strap might make it feel as if you don't look worth robbing,' he'd said. 'But seriously, darling…is that what these guys are after? And dressing like a ragamuffin doesn't make you any less a woman. You'll still be fair game in their eyes.'

Cheers, my love.

She clutched her mug, exhausted by fear and anxiety, weary of constantly looking over her shoulder and trying to second-guess the motives of every man who came close. Thomas Hallam was now doing fourteen years in prison. But she saw others like him everywhere; in all walks of life, at all times of day.

Are you saying they aren't out there?

The wind gusted outside, and something skittered along the windowpane. Pamela glanced around. The kitchen light showed a vortex of autumn leaves swirling in the garden.

She relaxed again. A little bit.

One step at a time, but yes it was true, at some point you actually had to take that step.

Tomorrow was the obvious occasion, but it wouldn't be easy.

Ironically, she'd been planning to carry a hammer in her handbag. Quite seriously, though purely for practical reasons.

Who knew, though, it might reassure her in other ways.

When morning came, Gerald, predictably, was grudging about it.

He bought her explanation that a window panel was loose and needed nailing in place until it could be fixed properly, and even went to the shed and got his claw-hammer, along with some nails. But he didn't look happy.

'Going the whole hog now, are we? Not just dressing like a bloke but acting like one too.'

These words played themselves through Pamela's mind again and again as the Merc pulled away, and she started up the path to the front door. But interestingly, they angered her as well as shamed her. And maybe that was good. Maybe it signaled that some of her old spirit was returning. Not that this mood of defiance lasted very long.

Because the man was waiting on the step.

Smiling as she approached.

He introduced himself as Alan Kyper and he immediately came over as the sort of chap a girl could take home to mother. He was somewhere in his mid-twenties, of average height and build, with soft, wavy fair hair and boyish looks. He dressed smartly too, wearing a Burberry trench coat over trousers, shoes and a checkerboard V-necked sweater, with a shirt and tie underneath—but from the outset, none of it added up.

Why's a young guy like this not doing a real job?

It occurred to her that he might be under the wrong impression about what would be required of him here. He had a large sports bag, after all, which was zipped closed.

So, what's in there, his murder kit?

But, he then put the bag in the Stock Room with his coat and chatted amiably with Pamela while she made coffee in the kitchen. He had a faint North Midlands accent, but it was soft and refined, and when he spoke, he articulated well.

'I guess you're wondering why I'm here?' he said, as though he'd been reading her thoughts.

Pamela threw him a guarded glance as she brewed. It wasn't a big room, but Kyper remained at the other side of it, maintaining a respectful distance.

'It's because I'm taking a brief sabbatical,' he said.

'Sabbatical?' She tried to maintain an air of indifference.

'There's a project I'm pursuing, which keeps me occupied in the evenings. It's quite demanding in that it needs a lot of focus and forward-planning. It also keeps me up until late each night.'

Are you actually hearing this?

'So, I thought it best if during the day I filled my time with...well, something less challenging. No offence, by the way.'

Pamela shrugged.

'That's why I've come to Manchester. It's a big change of scene for me, but it's taken me out of my normal social group, and that's the point. It means there are less distractions.'

'So, you've only moved to the area recently?' she couldn't help but ask.

'Last June.'

Christ in a cartoon!

Pamela said nothing.

'Since then, I've been, well...' He smiled sheepishly. 'Kicking my heels, mostly. Familiarizing myself with the district. Going for walks, riding the bus routes. None of it very constructive. Which is why I started looking for something real to do. I spotted this operation, which, now I'm here, feels as if it'll be absolutely ideal.'

'We don't get very busy, I'm afraid,' Pamela said.

'I understand that. But at least I'm connecting with human beings again.'

He wasn't connecting with human beings when he was down in the Midlands?

'Hello?' someone called from the direction of the counter.

Pamela hurried down there, relieved, and was pleased to see Mr. Ogilvy with another of those cardboard boxes, this one also packed to bursting with paperbacks. He was a big man in his mid-fifties, with shaggy grey hair and a scraggy beard. As usual, he wore paint-stained surplus army pants and a baggy, dusty sweatshirt.

'Just wondering if you can make use of these,' he said, in a curter voice than usual.

'It's very kind of you,' Pamela said, as he pushed the box across the counter. 'I don't know what we'd do without contributions like these.'

Surprised by her pleasant tone, he glanced around, registering Mrs. Brody's absence. 'You alone here today?'

'You mean is Mrs. Brody around? No, she's not.'

In truth, Pamela was a little surprised that she was being so garrulous. Possibly, she was reacting to the discomforting presence of a stranger like Mr. Kyper by reaching out to the more familiar figure of Mr. Ogilvy. Either way, it felt nice.

'I'm sorry she was rude to you last time. That's just the way she is. But no, she's gone off to have her baby.'

'Aye, well…I expected that.' He shrugged. 'But no apology's needed. I know it wasn't you. Anyway…' he tapped the side of the box, 'there are just under two-hundred in here.'

'Good heavens!'

'I suppose you're wondering where they're all coming from, eh?'

'I was, rather…' Pamela found herself warming to him even more. Despite his bluff exterior, his ruggedness had a kind of fatherly appeal. Okay, he was scruffy, and his hands were covered in dust and grit, his fingernails marked underneath with what looked like wood-stain, but none of that mattered. They were a working man's hands. They implied integrity.

'Came down here from Stirling a few months ago, after my aunt died,' he explained. 'She was a second-hand book dealer in central Manchester. I inherited the business. But it wasn't very profitable. The premises were saleable of course, as was a lot of the stock—so, we sold it all. But then we discovered she had a cellar room in her house, which was loaded with more books. Most of them are in good nick, but I'm in a rush to clear the place, and it just seemed easier to give them all to charity.' Again, though a gruff sort, he seemed honest, genuine.

'Anyway, I must be off. I'll see you again when I've boxed the next few up.'

'Don't you want to take some in exchange?' Pamela said. '*I won't restrict you to three.*'

But he was already edging towards the door. 'I'm fine but thank you.'

She nodded and smiled, as the big Scotsman left.

'Friend of yours?' Mr. Kyper wondered from the staff corridor, where he'd been standing with coffee in hand.

How long's he been there? Why didn't he come out where Ogilvy could see him?

'No, but he's...erm, he's a regular,' Pamela said. 'He brings us lots of donations.'

He emerged and stood alongside her, peering down at the box of books. 'If everyone's that generous, we'll be going on forever.'

God forbid!

'Mr. Ogilvy's a bit of an exception,' Pamela said.

'Whatever...you have a lovely rapport with the customers, Pam. Is it okay if I call you Pam?'

Actually, she thought it a little forward of him. Something seemed to have changed in the last minute or so. He was smiling a little, but not quite so innocently, his lips open, his teeth apart. It was almost a leer, and though it was only slight, it made him seem marginally less deferential, less polite.

Use your noggin girl. He's just seen you flirting with a customer? And he's already clocked your wedding ring. That's how these guys gain leverage.

Though just as quickly, it seemed, he now regained his affable persona.

The real him is someone he'd rather keep hidden, isn't it?

'I'll take these through to the kitchen, Pam.' He picked up his empty coffee mug. 'Then, shall I put Ogilvy's contributions on the shelves?'

'Please, that'd be great,' she said. 'Oh, and...I'd prefer

Pamela, if you don't mind.'

I bet you'd also prefer him to say Mister Ogilvy, eh? But perhaps best not to go there.

'Sure thing.' He smiled pleasantly again. 'Pamela, it is.'

She felt frustrated with herself as she listened to him clattering about in the kitchen, and then start the taps running. Okay, she'd been determined to be strong today, and to use this new period of having to work with someone she didn't know as the turning-point, as the way back to normality. But while attack was the best form of defense, wasn't she making things a little hard for herself? There was no need to feel so hostile to this guy.

Yes, he'd seemed a little bumptious a couple of minutes ago, but that had been fleeting. Generally, he'd been amicable—and helpful, which was more than she could say for Gerald.

Isn't there something about him, though? Why does he make you feel so uncomfortable?

'He doesn't,' she said aloud. 'It's just that I don't know him yet. He's only just got here. It's a weird situation.'

Even then, she felt as if she wasn't being totally honest, but had to bite her lip further as Mr. Kyper re-emerged from the corridor.

'Oh,' he said. 'Sorry...I thought someone else had come in.'

'No.' She tried to smile. 'Just muttering to myself.'

'I do that too.' He lifted the counter hatch. 'A lot.'

So did Thomas Hallam.

Pamela watched as he breezed through into the Library, carrying the box of books as if it contained nothing more than fluff. There was internal arched window on her right, which gave through into the same area. It meant that she could still keep an eye on him as he dumped the box on the coffee table, pulled up a chair, and begin working his way through the contributions, arranging them into orderly piles. One, he picked up and looked at more closely. She saw that leering grin again. He turned the book around to read the blurb, and then started flicking through its pages. A minute or so passed before he stood up, placing the paperback on top of the nearest pile, swooped that pile up and ambled over to the *Thrillers* section. One by one, he slotted the books into place.

You could really do with knowing which book it was that interested him so much.

Pamela couldn't help it; she made a mental note to check once he'd moved away, which he did a short time later, walking back to the table, picking up another pile and heading off in a different direction. She came out from behind the counter and idled into the Library. He was already at the far end of the room, back turned as he worked his way along the *Romance* shelves. She made an immediate beeline for *Thrillers*, eyes fixed on the spine of the book in question. It would be something daft, she was sure. He'd been laughing at something silly. She might even be amused herself. So thinking, she yanked the item out.

It was called: *Jack the Knife*.

Its cover depicted a leather-gloved hand holding a bloodstained blade to a heaving cleavage.

It purported to be: *The absolute final word on the Jack the Ripper murders*.

Pamela spent twenty minutes in late-morning in the Stock Room, hammering nails through the frame of the loose window panel. She didn't have much expertise, so a couple of the nails went askew, and she struck one of the others so hard that the glass cracked. She wasn't unduly worried. Of far greater concern was the situation out *there*, with Alan Kyper.

After identifying the book, she'd struggled just to face him again.

He appeared not to notice her tense behavior, and after putting all the new books into their rightful places, chatted on for the next hour or so, mainly about nothing. One or two customers came in, and he dealt with them efficiently. A young, studious-looking woman had a bagful of battered old Mills & Boons and asked if they had a copy of *The Town and the City* by Jack Kerouac, which she could take away in exchange. Pamela wouldn't have known where to start, but Alan guided the woman straight to *Modern Classics*, where, though they didn't find *The Town and the City*, he made her happy by giving her a copy of *The Dharma Bums*, its original 1958 cover only mildly creased. The lady thanked him profusely as he then accompanied her to the door, talking about Kerouac's work intelligently and interestingly.

That was the point when Pamela went to fix the window, loudly explaining that it needed to be done, because though *Book-a-Thon* received an annual grant from the Council, running costs were always tight. It was colder outside now, and they couldn't afford to let warm air just drain away. He shrugged, as though it made sense but seemed puzzled that she'd felt the need to explain this to him. Another customer then came in, and he immediately and ingratiatingly took charge of her. Pamela withdrew, not just unnerved by the conundrum that was their new staff member, but feeling a little surplus to requirements.

Doesn't surprise you that he's a show-off, does it? They are all about ego, these fellas. That's what that psychiatrist bloke said on the news the other night. Before you panicked and left the room.

When Pamela re-emerged later, it was almost noon and Mr. Banks came in, pulling off his woolen gloves as he hunched towards the counter.

Immediately, she realized that she'd made a mistake.

The old man was here to read the dailies, but Mrs. Brody had always been the one to bring the newspapers in. Pamela could have done that this morning, but she'd been so keyed up that it had never entered her head. Providing newspapers wasn't really part of the *Book-a-Thon* service, but they were at the heart of a community drive here—there were all sorts of leaflets and posters about other events and services—and the thinking had always been that any reason to get people in would be a good one.

The old man looked disappointed when she broke the news, seeming only mildly placated by her promise that she wouldn't forget tomorrow.

'Police everywhere out there,' he grunted. 'Never seen so many. Cars on every corner, bobbies going door-to-door. Not much good now though…with the lass dead'

'Hopefully the fact they're out there will prevent any more attacks,' Pamela replied.

'I wouldn't count on that,' someone interrupted. It was Mr. Kyper. He'd just seen another satisfied customer to the door, and now ambled to the counter to join them. 'Serial killers don't tend to stop until they get caught. I mean, they're hunted by the law wherever they go, but often it doesn't even slow them down. It's like it's a vocation for them.'

Mr. Banks eyed him curiously. 'Well…I hope they catch this bugger soon. No good for Brookshaw, you know. Anyway…' he sighed and pulled his gloves on, 'I'll be on my way.'

He turned and lumbered out.

'I must say, you're all taking it pretty well,' Mr. Kyper said. 'On the whole.'

'I'm sorry?' Pamela replied.

'The cops are up and down these streets like boy-racers, but everyone else in Brookshaw seems pretty relaxed about the murders.'

'Well…there's only been *one* here, hasn't there?'

'Two if you count that student, Sarah Galloway.'

'That was on the outskirts of town,' Pamela said. 'Halfway to Bury.'

He seemed unimpressed by the argument. 'None of the four have actually been that far from *here*. I'm sorry, but Brookshaw feels like Ground Zero to me.'

'Ground Zero?'

He leaned on the counter. 'There's a theory in criminal psychology that serial killers only hunt in areas they're familiar with. That's not just so they can make quick getaways. It's because it's their turf…you know, their domain.'

Pamela was too uncomfortable with the subject to keep discussing it. 'Let's hope he gets caught soon.'

'Though, of course, it could be somewhere they've staked out. You know, somewhere they've travelled to…like a foreign land they wish to conquer.'

Christ's sake, he's all but coughing to it.

Pamela was tempted to leave the premises there and then. But Mr. Kyper moved back into the Library, where he seemed content to remain, dealing with those few customers who came in, again affecting a charming manner and proving knowledgeable about books and writers.

In so many ways, that was just the kind of thing they needed here…

He's plausible, for sure. But isn't that something else the TV shrink said you should look out for? Plausibility.

But plausible or not, he was undeniably useful. He happily volunteered to stay on while Pamela retired to the kitchen to warm a Pot Noodle.

As she sat at the kitchen table and ate, she again told herself that she'd behaved ridiculously. Even that awful book, *Jack the Knife*, had caused her to overreact. The cover was horrible, but most likely that was because it dated from a different, less tasteful era.

And he'd found it funny.

Or maybe he hadn't. Maybe he'd just been amused by the lurid thoughtlessness of it.

This reminded her that he'd erroneously put that book into *Thrillers*, when it should be in with *True Crime*. She'd move it at the first opportunity but didn't want to do that while Kyper was watching.

You mean he might feel slighted? That he'll have an actual reason to cut you up?

No immediate opportunity arose.

After Pamela had returned to the counter, Kyper ate a sandwich, but did so while seated in the Library. Outside meanwhile, a very autumnal day was manifesting. Spatters of rain hit the windows, leaves twirling by. A sky, which had been grey and heavy from first thing, deepened in tone. By 3 p.m. they'd had to turn the lights on. No more customers came in.

'You can tell the hour's gone back,' he commented, wandering to the counter. 'It's getting dark already, and it's not four yet.'

Pamela acknowledged this with a nod.

'Don't think we've had anyone in for the last hour,' he said.

'It's usually better on Saturdays,' she replied.

'All these books. I'm tempted to have a browse. But if I start now, I'll likely never stop.'

'I don't think there's any harm having a browse,' she said, hoping that it would make him leave her alone. 'And if you see something you fancy, just take it…'

Could have used better terminology there, girl.

'I mean,' she added quickly, 'we're donating our time being here, so it's not as if you haven't earned the right to take a couple of books.'

He mused on that. 'There are other things I could do with my time while I'm here…if that's acceptable? I mean, as long as there are no customers in.'

She shrugged.

'I'll have a browse first, though.' He moved away. 'Like you say. Can't do any harm.'

Pamela sidled to the arched window to watch. If he'd made a beeline for *Jack the Knife*, she wasn't sure how she'd feel. But instead, he had a general wander, checking casually along various other shelves.

Perhaps it was time to remove temptation altogether.

That vile book ought to go in *True Crime*, but maybe the best place for it was the bin.

Yeah. You never know…it might demoralize him so much that he stops killing.

'Shut up,' she muttered, strolling into the Library, and, noting that his back was turned, shooting quickly over to *Thrillers*, snatching the offending item from its perch.

Gingerly, she leafed through the pages as she took it back behind the counter. If it was a decent piece of writing—a scholarly work rather than garish titillation—she might grant it a stay. But if not…she halted, shocked, when she saw that someone, a previous owner, had gone to work on it with a pencil, inscribing notes in the margins, even underlining certain passages. Movement drew her eye to the arched window, where Kyper was walking back across the Library. Hastily, she took the book down the staff corridor and ducked into the toilets. There were two cubicles in there, and she locked herself into the second one, lowering the lid and sitting. Increasingly fearful, she flipped the pages again.

Some bits of text had been underlined with such force that the paper had torn.

…throat cut so savagely that the windpipe was completely severed…

…disembowled, the guts arrayed around her in a gory pattern…

Pamela fought to tell herself that this was the work of some silly teenager, some daft kid who'd got childishly excited by gore. But then, another sentence that had been underlined almost made her choke.

…. recently released from a lunatic asylum…

Her thoughts strayed back to Kyper.

What was that term he used…that he 'wasn't connecting with human beings'? Obviously not, if he was cooped up in a nut-hatch.

She had to violently fight down her panic.

This book was nothing to do with Alan Kyper. He'd only handled the thing for a moment. After that, she'd kept an eye on him, and he hadn't been anywhere near the *Thrillers* shelves.

Apart from when you went off and nailed that window closed.

New fear gripped her. But again, with a little common sense, she was able to get on top of it. These pencil marks were old and faded. They couldn't be anything to do with Kyper.

But could they be evidence of some other sort?

Might the police be interested?

She tried rejecting that idea too, telling herself that it was an old book—it dated from the 1970s, in fact—about a completely different series of murders. The fact that someone had shown an unusual degree of interest in the graphic nature of the crimes would not be unusual either. It could have been one of these so-called 'Ripperologists'—ghoulish old men for the most part, she suspected—who continued to investigate the case from their armchairs.

Feeling a little more relaxed, she flicked more pages. If there was a name scribbled in here, maybe, or even a date of ownership, then maybe that would put her mind at ease…

Instead, she found a final note from the author:

It is my conviction that, thanks literally to the nickname he was given, Jack the Ripper lives in criminal eternity. Whether he chose that name himself or was christened thus by a journalist looking to blow the story up into something much larger than a mundane murder case, we shall never know. But it wasn't the only name he went by; there were numerous others. For a brief time, he was known as 'the Whitechapel Murderer'.

Then, after the Catherine Eddowes slaying, the newspapers called him 'Leather Apron'. In the immediate decades following the case, children of the East End created their own names. One of these, initially part of a chant to accompany a skipping-rope game, afterwards became immortalized in the canon of Cockney rhyming slang:

Mr. Kipper—Jack the Ripper
Jack the Ripper—Mr. Kipper

Mr. Kipper.
Pamela turned so cold and faint that, if she hadn't been sitting, she'd have fallen.
Mr. Kipper...
And a couple of rooms away in this same building, there was a man called...
Mr. Kyper...

It had to be coincidence. Pamela told herself this repeatedly as she sat on the toilet lid. It wasn't as if his parents had named him in anticipation of his growing up to be a murderer.
Suppose he's given himself this name?
That was a valid point.
Book-a-Thon was a community project, not a company or charity where they had rules and regulations about making background checks on people they employed. Kyper wasn't even officially employed. He could be anyone who'd walked off the street, having given himself any name he liked.
If you can just get to your phone...it's in your bag on the counter.
Pamela stood up stiffly. But then had to check herself. What was she talking about...'if she could get to her phone'?
Of course she could get to her phone. And when she got to it, who was she going to call? Gerald? He'd merely tell her to

get a grip.

How about the police, genius?

But even that didn't seem like a plan. No doubt they were buried under work, those hundred detectives allegedly working the case, chasing every lead, their bosses running wild at headquarters as the public clamor grew.

Maybe for that reason alone, they'll want to come and check this guy?

On reflection, it *was* possible. This would hardly be an urgent line of enquiry, but if they were leaving no stone unturned…

Okay, she'd call the police.

It wouldn't make her life easy afterwards. If Kyper turned out to be completely innocent, it would be difficult continuing to work here with him, though like as not, he wouldn't want to stay anyway, and if he did, Pamela wouldn't. It was that simple.

Closing the book as quietly as she could, though its pages seemed to rustle inordinately loudly, she left it on the cistern lid, and leaned towards the door to listen. There was no sound. She checked her watch—it was almost five, thank Heaven—and yet she was so deep inside the building that she couldn't even hear the evening traffic. Not that this mattered. Kyper didn't know that she suspected him yet. All she had to do was walk back to the counter, rummage in her bag, and walk here back again. He wouldn't think anything of it.

Unless, he's already spotted that you took this book from the shelf.

Pamela hovered there, flesh tingling.

But even then, why would he worry? He couldn't know that she'd used it to connect him to the crimes.

Nervously, she unlocked the cubicle—again it echoed and re-echoed—and then moved to the toilet door, ears straining.

Still, nothing.

She poked her head out.

At the Library end of the corridor, she saw the back of the

counter. In the other direction, the Stock Room door stood ajar. There was no sign of movement either way.

Is he lying in wait somewhere?

Again, why would he? Just supposing he was exactly what she feared, why would he attack someone here, where he was lying low? That would blow his cover.

True, but maybe he suspects that you've twigged him?

Still not seeing how that was possible, Pamela forced herself out. Her phone was no more than twenty yards away. All she had to do was grab it, bring it back…

'I know I won't be able to resist this one,' a male voice said, somewhere behind her.

Pamela turned slowly towards the Stock Room door.

Don't even ask if that was him. Who else could it be?

But it had sounded so different. Gone was the casual tone. Gone was the easy, conversational style. Suddenly, he'd sounded intense, driven. And who was he talking to?

He's on the phone, obviously.

'Soon as I get the chance, I'm going to do it,' he said.

Pamela felt faint with nausea.

He's got an accomplice. Isn't that what they said about the original Ripper? That there might've been two of them?

'It'll be risky…and I won't do it now,' he said. 'I've got to build up some credibility first. But I won't be able to resist forever, and the longer I wait the better it's going to be. When I've finished with this one, she'll look like something off the back shelf of the butcher's…'

Pamela clamped a hand onto her mouth before squealing aloud. She wobbled where she stood, still thinking she was going to collapse, her weight travelling from one foot to the other—and a rogue floorboard creaking in response.

The silence in the Stock Room was instant and eerie.

You know he just heard that, don't you?

Feet thudded towards the door, and it opened inward—but Pamela had already tottered into the toilets, where she slid into the same cubicle as previously, closing the door again and bolting it.

Feet came along the corridor. Inevitably, they halted outside.

Pamela hung onto her breath desperately, vison blurred with tears of terror.

The utter silence lingered.

If he stuck his head in here, he'd see the cubicle locked, but might he just assume that she was answering nature's call?

Get real! You know what he is, so do you think he'll take a chance?

To Pamela's surprise, however, she now heard more footfalls, and these were receding along the corridor towards the counter.

He's only going to check that no one's come in. To make sure there are no witnesses.

Pamela didn't wait to hear more. She tottered out into the corridor, and without even looking behind her, stumbled towards the Stock Room. If she could get the window open, she could shout for help to the Mothers & Babies Club. Someone would hear her.

But only when she jumped up onto the stool and saw the row of flat nail-heads along the bottom of the frame did she realize the futility of that ambition. She grabbed the hammer from the windowsill and tried to claw the offending articles loose. Splinters and paint-chips flew as she inexpertly rent at the wood, so consumed with panic that she didn't hear the door swing open again.

She didn't even realize he was there until she sensed that he was right at her back.

'Pamela, I don't know what you think you're doing...' He chuckled as he leaned past, reaching to take the hammer off her. 'But that's not going to help you...'

With a shriek, she spun around, swinging the tool as hard as she could, cracking it against his left temple with such force that she felt something give.

'…your…with your running…costs…' His words came out a burble, as he staggered backwards, mouth fixed in a surprised grin, blood swimming in a crimson torrent down his left cheek. A second of apparent stupefaction passed before he crashed sideways onto the small table, upending his open sports bag, its contents cascading to the floor.

Pamela was initially frozen, peering down confusedly at his prone figure, and the chaos of pens, notebooks, and other paperwork now heaped all over him.

'Mr.…Mr. Kyper?' She climbed warily down, her whole body shaking.

He didn't respond.

He's not going to, is he? He's going to play dead until you're within reach.

But he didn't look as if he was playing. Even the pool of blood on the carpet tiles looked to be congealing. She couldn't see any sign of breathing.

He couldn't be? Surely not…?

Best if he is.

Her gaze fell on his left hand, in which his mobile phone was cradled. Though…now that she looked more closely, it wasn't a phone.

She risked leaning down further, and a thrill of shock went through her as she recognized a Dictaphone. She knew that because Mr. Bagwell, who she'd worked for in Manchester, had used one. Kyper hadn't been talking to an accomplice, but to himself.

Keeping a record of his misdeeds.

That's a serial killer. Aren't they notorious for collecting trophies?

Pamela's first emotion after that was strained relief. If she'd really hurt him badly, it wouldn't matter, because here was the proof of what he was. She turned to his spilled paperwork for further evidence. She picked up a notebook and flipped it open.

And had to make a double-take.

MY OTHER SELF
A crime thriller
by Alan Kyper

She didn't bother reading through the scribbled paragraphs underneath. An acidic sensation ate through her as she grabbed up more notebooks and opened those, seeing more chapter headings, more hand-written notes, instructions in the margins, like: 'For monologue, chap 3, use dictaphone.' Frantic, she snatched a sheet of paper, and saw that it was a printed email, from someone called Mervin...who was literary agent.

'Thanks, Merv,' Kyper had written in an earlier missive, copied in at the bottom. 'I've moved up to Manchester for the duration of this investigation. Need to know what it's like in a town where a real killer's on the loose. Hopefully, will give my new novel the authenticity the others have lacked. May get his one published...'

The next thing Pamela knew, she was stumbling down the corridor, hyperventilating.

She had to get to her phone, but not to call the police this time. To call an ambulance. No sooner had she lurched to the counter, though, than a figure loomed on the other side.

A large, burly figure, with a beetroot complexion.

Pamela was stricken dumb with shock—until she recognized Mr. Ogilvy.

She might have felt terrible, but he didn't look great, himself. He was bug-eyed, sweating, his grizzled cheeks tinged crimson.

'Thank God you're still open,' he panted. 'I need to reclaim one of those books I dropped off this morning. It's an old family Bible and it's of great personal value. I brought it along by accident. So, do you mind if I go and get it back...?'

'I, erm...'

Pamela couldn't reply, her mouth was too dry, though he seemed to take this as a 'yes', thanking her and striding into the Library.

Out of the frying pan, eh?

Pamela shuddered uncontrollably, fresh sweat streaming as she lumbered to the arched window to watch him.

What a give-away that pencil is, eh?

It was inserted behind his ear. She knew that lots of working men did that, but to then come charging back here, anxious to retrieve a family Bible...?

The Bible really gets people running around in a lather, these days, doesn't it?

This was Mr. Ogilvy, she tried to tell herself.

The same guy who earlier today was interested to learn that you were alone here?

But we know him...

You've only known him the last four months. Which is roughly the time of...

Pamela tried not to listen, but as she watched the big Scot mooching along the shelves, she reached slowly for her coat. It was impossible to think of him as anything other than a nice man.

They're always plausible, remember?

That didn't matter. When he found that Bible, it would be okay.

And when he doesn't find it, the book he's really looking for—because it's back there in the toilets, you dope—what do you think will happen then?

'It's not Mr. Ogilvy,' she chuntered. 'It can't be.'

Let's hope your instinct's working better now than it was with poor Kyper.

Pamela almost sobbed aloud. Kyper was still lying back there. But she couldn't do anything to help him. She suddenly couldn't do anything at all...just stand here, frozen, watching, waiting...

Waiting for the inevitable? How about that wood-stain under Ogilvy's fingernails? Oh, you're on form today, dar-

ling.

Coat now on but still semi-petrified, Pamela continued to watch the man. At any second, she expected to see him glance round, realize that she was about to flee, and come bounding across the Library. But he didn't. He still seemed keen to locate his missing book.

Wouldn't you, if it could put you away for thirty years.

There was no argument. Pamela would have to chance the streets outside, even though full darkness had now fallen. But still she couldn't move—until, by what seemed like a miracle of timing, the headlights of Gerald's Merc slid to a halt at the end of the path.

It broke the spell.

Thanks to God flooded out of her in a wail, as she grabbed her bag from the counter, threw the hatch open and rushed for the glass door, stepping outside, pulling it closed behind her, and firmly locking it.

She backed away down the path, her attention focused on the building. There was still no visible movement. Ogilvy was doubtless searching in vain for the book that would condemn him. While Kyper…poor Alan Kyper…

Despair welled up as Pamela recalled the writer's lifeless body. She didn't know whether they'd go easy on her due to these unique circumstances. Though if that young man was dead, she'd never be able to forgive herself. She opened the passenger door and flopped into the passenger seat, tears streaming down her face as the truth of her own ineptitude swept over her. Predictably, there was a sigh from the driver's seat.

'Can we just drive.' Pamela's tear-blurred vision remained on the building. 'Just get us away from here…there's a phone call I have to make. It's very urgent.'

They pulled from the curb as she rooted in her bag—where, rather than her own personals, she found three hefty textbooks. The first, *The Enlightenment*, fell open in her lap.

Streetlight and shadow flickered kaleidoscopically over the first page, where a beautifully handwritten note read:

To my darling Sarah
In recognition of her great achievement.
Hope you enjoy Manchester Uni.
XXX Grandma

She'd picked up the wrong cloth bag from the counter. But that name—Sarah?

Sarah Galloway? The Manchester University student who'd...

'You didn't need to bring those back. They were a gift.'

Pamela looked slowly, disbelievingly around.

The truth was, she ought to have realized straight away that she wasn't in Gerald's Mercedes. It smelled smoky and dank, and it had got here several minutes earlier than usual. But she still hadn't expected that husky young man in denims, the one with the longish hair and moustache.

'We were trying to do some good,' he said, as he drove them at great speed through the night.

'We?' she whispered.

He didn't reply. But someone else did. Someone lurking behind the shabby curtain that separated them from the transit van's rear. Whoever it was, he chuckled, before dragging her backwards into that dark, foul space.

I told you there were two of them.

Pamela shrieked.

Don't say I didn't warn you.

HALF INCH
Inspired by the Rhyming Slang for Pinch...as in to Steal
Jay Stringer

"How would you do it?" Megan said, letting him see the smile.

Jimmy Finch met her eyes, "This place?"

She bent down and sucked iced latte up through the straw, "Uh huh."

Jimmy took a look around the diner, pretending like he hadn't already done it.

The diner was wide, split into two sections, with the kitchen through a hatch at the back, behind the counter. The cash register was in the center of the room, on a wooden stand, like a lectern. There were eight customers, including Jimmy and Megan. Three couples, and two people on their own.

Nobody was reading a newspaper. That was the biggest change from when Jimmy started out. There would always be a couple people reading newspapers. Now it's all cell phones. Everyone has a camera, and a way to call the cops.

"Well, there's only two servers working. One for that side, one for this side. They keep meeting in the middle, at the register, to talk. They've looked over our way a bunch of times, so they think we're on a date."

"Really?" Megan turned now to look at them, seeing them standing together. Her voice rose, just a little. "That's what they think?"

"Sure. Young attractive woman like you, flirting with an older guy like me."

"I'm *not* flirting."

"The problem here is, their attention is already on us. I mean, they've been aware of us since we came in, they've talked about us a bunch. If I was to try anything in here, they'd notice me sooner than anyone else, more likely to stop it. Plus, they'd remember me to the cops, describe me, you. We'd get caught too easy."

"Okay," Megan's tone was colder now, the playfulness gone. "Obviously, I don't mean how would you do it right now, in this meeting. But if this was one of your jobs, you walk in for the first time, how would you do it?"

Jimmy leaned back in his seat, looked Megan up and down. This Hollywood producer with an option out on his story. No, not producer. He couldn't remember what. She'd told him her job title a bunch of times, and it had the word *producer* in it, but he wasn't sure she had any actual responsibility.

"You're looking for the ending to the movie."

Megan leaned forward, "Of course I am, we got nothing right now."

Jimmy put his hand on the manuscript between them, his autobiography, *Pinch: The Story of the Joke Bandit*. Optioned before publication. "I robbed two hundred and thirty-seven places. At least one in every state. All but one of them unarmed, walking out with money without ever pointing a gun. Only served time for *one* of them, you can't find a story?"

"It's not the story that's the problem, it's the ending. Every writer we get on this tanks, tells us the same thing, there's no ending. Your book gives us you, but that's not enough. We know your past, we know the jobs you did, we know the prison stuff, but then you get out and…what? Where do we roll credits?"

"You want me to pull another job."

"It would give us an ending."

"But I've gone straight, so you're stuck."

"Maybe you don't need to actually do the job, maybe you're just thinking about it. That could be the scene. Yeah, I can see it." She shuffled into the middle of the booth, directly across from him, putting her hands up on either side of her face, making an imaginary camera lens. "You're in a diner, like this one, or a different one. We make it look just typical of all the places you robbed earlier in the film."

"This place is pretty typical."

"Right, so you're sitting here, and we've had the build-up of you going straight. How you've come out of prison a changed man, but we also show that you're tempted, that you can't just switch off who you are. Then someone says to you, *how would you do it?*"

"Who?"

"In the scene? I don't know. Doesn't matter yet, we'll think of somebody."

"So it could be in the middle of a date?"

"We are *not* on a date."

"No, but in the movie."

"So this person, okay, let's say it's a date. Maybe, what's the name of that woman on your last job, the one made you carry the gun?"

"Lisa."

"So, maybe it's Lisa."

"She's dead."

"Sure, but she doesn't need to be. Not for the story. It could be the two of you talking. That's how we frame it. That's how we frame the whole thing, we *start* on this scene, the two of you meeting up after years apart, start talking, then we flash back into your life, and we show that Lisa's always been the temptation, right? Then at the end, we cut back to this scene, and maybe she doesn't say *how would you do it*, maybe it's more like she says, *so, are you ready?* Then we close in on your face, like this." She moves her hands in closer. "Let the audience see you thinking about it, just long enough, then cut to black."

"That's your idea for the ending?"

"I think it could be pretty cool, arty like, you know? People love that."

"They don't actually see me doing the job, though?"

"Don't need to. They know you're going to. Or maybe some think you don't. They can decide for themselves, like that spinning top thing in the dream movie."

"I hated that."

"Point is, we've given them an ending to the story."

"Why can't this be the ending? Just sitting here talking, on a date."

"We're not—"

"Or the real ending. You've got the book. Can't we just end where the book does?"

"You walking out of prison? Terrible ending. What's the structure there? What's the punch? What are we asking the audience to take away?"

"I'm not asking them to take anything away, that's the truth of it, that's where my story ends."

"Unless..." Megan was back into pitch mode again. "Unless we see you walking out, you've just had some exchange with the warden where he says, *see you soon* and you say no, you're done, you're going straight. Then we see you walk out, right, and...we hear a car coming...and then we see Lisa pull up in front of you. She smiles, just smiles, but we know what it means, and then we see you smile, fade to black. Or better, *cut* to black. Instant."

"Feels a bit too much like a crime movie."

"We're *making* a crime movie."

"They're always fake. You're just making the same thing over and over. If that's all you wanted to do, why not just go do that, you didn't need my book."

"No, we wanted your book, we wanted *you*, your story. That's what the viewer wants, too. Real life, you know?"

"But you want to change it."

"Movies have certain rules, like a language, a different language. We need to hit certain beats, because that's what people expect."

"Like this thing you've got for Lisa. 'She represents the temptation'." Jimmy made air quotes. "Like I need *temptation*. Or the last writer you hooked me up with, said he wanted to get to the heart of my story, and I said, well, here's the book. And he goes, no, I want to know why you did it, why you decided to rob those places."

Megan looked down at her notes on the table, and Jimmy guessed that was the next item on the agenda.

"You need to make some big scene in the movie about me being tempted, or something that makes me commit the crime, you want me to rationalize it. You want to know why I robbed places?"

Megan's face lit up. "Yeah."

"Because I'm a criminal, and good at it. Lisa didn't *tempt* me into anything. It was a job. She knew I didn't use guns, but offered me more money, and I said yes. That's not *temptation*, it's a job offer."

"So *money* was the temptation."

"Is money the temptation for what you do? We need to try and figure out the deep motivation for why you're in this job."

"I love working on movies."

"There you go. We both like what we do."

"What you *did*. Now that you're straight. What are you planning to do? Maybe we can work that into the movie, like a redemption arc?"

Jimmy wasn't paying attention. He was busy watching a new customer. Small and wiry, wearing an army castoff jacket. One of those German ones with the flag still on the sleeve.

He'd been seated over this side, a few booths over. Jimmy had watched as the guy scoped the place out, the same way he did.

This guy was *impossible.*

Megan Quinn wanted to call her boss, just say, "We can't do this, let's make a different movie." But she couldn't. You didn't get to run your own movie that way. She figured, get good information from Jimmy Finch, get good *story*, and she could make this into her ticket.

But now he wasn't even paying attention.

"Hello?"

Jimmy's eyes shifted back to her. He didn't apologize.

Megan was like, really?

So rude. So sure of himself. Just sitting there, not interested in explaining himself, not interested in telling his story. Who does that? Who doesn't want to talk about themselves?

Megan looked down at her notes. The list of issues given to her by the writer and studio. All the things they needed to fix to make the book into a film. A couple of the notes had come from the publisher, too. Over a coffee the day before, his editor has said, "Hey, we're having the same issues, maybe if you can get him to talk, we can change the book."

Three hundred and forty pages, and nowhere did he explain himself, nowhere did he give any kind of justification. And that ending? What was that? The guy just walks out of prison and smells fresh air and that's *it*?

"Okay," Megan said, swirling the straw around in her now-empty glass. "Lets' talk about the jokes."

"You want to hear them?"

"No, I've read the book."

"They're not all in there, I got a bunch you won't have heard."

"Jimmy, I don't want to hear the jokes, I want to know why you told them."

Jimmy cocks his head, like he's never heard that question before. He looks like a confused puppy for a second. This guy in his late fifties, gray hair. In good shape for his age, but nowhere near as much as his self-confidence suggested.

"Who doesn't want to hear jokes?"

This was good, this was her way in. "I would think, people being robbed don't want to hear jokes. Cashiers don't want to hear them. Servers don't want to hear them."

Again with his confused look. Megan could tell now he was doing it for show. "They're the exact people who need them. You got to put people at ease if you're robbing them, make them relax, let them know things are okay, they don't need to do anything rash."

Megan looked down at her notes, *why not guns?*

"Okay, but tell me how that started? I mean, most people would just use a gun. You walk into places, up the register, and start telling a joke. Why not just point a gun, or pretend you're pointing a gun?"

"I don't like guns."

Megan felt the frustration rise again, her voice rising. "There has to be more to it."

"Why? Why you need more than that, I don't like guns, so I don't use them. I like jokes, so I tell them. You walk in, you spot the person most amenable, and you start talking to them, engage with them. Nice and friendly. You're telling them a joke, and while you do it, you hand them the sign that says, 'this is a robbery, give me all the money in the drawer.' You're still telling them the joke, so they're off balance, their brains going in two different ways. But everybody likes jokes, so they're still relaxed, deep down."

"You said find the person most *amenable*, how do you know?"

"It's just a sense, you have it or you don't."

Jimmy's eyes drift again. He keeps looking at something over her shoulder.

Megan isn't used to this kind of behavior. In these meetings, everyone wants to focus on her, to answer her, to work with her and be important.

Maybe the jokes are the way? Maybe it's in his childhood? He skips over that in the book.

"Okay, so let's talk about the jokes then, you like them so much. When did that start? Was it maybe a defense mechanism at school? We could frame it that way, show you using humor to get out of trouble, as a kid, you know?"

Jimmy rolled his eyes, looked at her again. "You want to make a crime movie, but you don't want to make a movie about criminals."

"But at school…"

"I tell jokes because I like them. Because I loved watching Johnny Carson, and I figured being him was the best thing in the world."

"Why not try being a comedian?"

"I wanted to make money."

Megan made a couple notes on the page. That was a good line. It wasn't much, this angle, but maybe they could use it. Show him as a frustrated comic, build up that way. She could see it, now she was thinking it. Early scenes, watching Carson. Maybe a flashback.

Yeah, it could work.

She looked at the next question.

"So, this Marshal who arrested you…"

Jimmy's eyes opened up. "Deputy US Marshal Chloe Medina."

Was that a *smile*? It was.

His focus was full on her now.

Megan tapped the notes, *bingo*. "Yeah. Tell me about her."

"She didn't shoot me." He paused, leaned back in the seat. "I mean, she could've shot me. She shot Lisa. But she didn't shoot me."

"Why do you think that was?"

"You should ask her."

We've tried, Megan thought. They'd tried to do a deal with Medina already, use her name, put her in the story. She refused both, they were going to have to change the name if they used the scene in the film. Someone else who didn't want to be in a movie. What was wrong with the world?

"Tell me what happened."

Jimmy shrugged. "Not much to it. We've gone in the bank. I hated doing banks, but Lisa had this idea. And she's got me packing, and I hated packing. But it's all working, this trick she had, knew the exact time the manager was opening this small safe they had behind the desk, like a drop box they put money before taking it all out the back? Lisa knew the exact time of day they opened it, and we'd got bags full of cash. We come out, and there's this Marshal standing there on the steps, just watching us."

"You knew what she was?"

"Well, you could tell she was something. Some kind of law."

"And she pulls a gun?"

"She's got her hand on the gun. On her hip. Which, by the way? Hottest thing I've ever seen. I mean, I don't like guns, but she made it work. And she identifies herself, says, 'Deputy US Marshal Chloe Medina, don't do anything stupid.' But then Lisa does something stupid."

"She tries to shoot her."

"Well, I guess. Her hand twitched. Lisa's gun was down at her side, we'd both lowered them as we came out the bank, thinking we didn't need them. Lisa's hand twitched. Not even an inch, really, and Chloe shot her. She drew so fast."

Chloe.

Megan was right. Jimmy had a thing for this Marshal.

"Then she looks at me, just looks at me, cocks an eyebrow, and I drop the gun. So yeah, she could've shot me, and she didn't."

"The one time you got caught."

"The one time."

"Love story between a criminal and a Marshal," Megan said, circling Medina's name in the notes. "There's a story there."

Jimmy didn't answer. He was gone again, focusing on something behind her.

She turned to look. A small guy in an army surplus jacket was standing at the register, pointing a gun at the two servers. He looked twitchy, nervous.

The gunman called out, "Nobody move."

Jimmy leaned forward. "That's not how I would do it."

The kid in the jacket looked scared. His gun pointing one way, then another.

"All the money," he was saying. "All of it."

The older of the two servers, the middle-aged woman with red hair, said, "Where you want us to put it?"

He didn't have a bag. Hadn't thought that far ahead.

Jimmy figured the kid hadn't even intended to rob the place. Just came in, maybe for a coffee, maybe to get off the street. But the gun in his pocket had made a stupid decision, and there was no way this ended well.

Jimmy slid out of the booth. He saw Mega turn to him, panicked, mouthing for him to stop. The kid spun halfway round, towards him. Jimmy looked at all the other customers, none of them sure what to do next, nobody having any idea what to do when a gun shows up.

"Freeze," the kid's voice going up a level. "Stop effing moving."

Effing? Jimmy put his hands out, palms up, and smiled. "I got you, I'm staying right here."

"Get back," the kid took a few steps towards him.

Jimmy watched the thoughts pass across the servers faces, was this their chance to do something?

"What I'm thinking," Jimmy said, "is that everybody should keep still."

"I *already* said that," the kid was whiny now. "But *somebody* didn't listen."

"I just want to help, give you some on-the-job training."

The kid pointed the gun square at Jimmy's face.

"I'm Jimmy Finch. You don't know me? Jimmy the Pinch? Nothing?"

"Uh…" A shrug. "No."

Jimmy took a small step forward. "Two hundred thirty-seven robberies, only caught one time. My date over there," he said, twitching his head, indicating Megan behind him, "is a Hollywood producer, going to make a movie based on me. So I'm basically an expert at what you're doing."

"Okay."

"How do you think you're doing right now?"

"Uh…" The kid looked at the two servers. They both shrugged. He turned back. "Okay?"

"I gotta be honest. This is not going well."

A flush of anger welled up in the kids face, but Jimmy read it for what it was, embarrassment. "No, man, I'm doing okay."

"You're scared, that's okay. You didn't plan on this, did you? Came in for some pancakes, maybe a coffee, a burger. You've had a bad day, right?"

The kid nodded.

Jimmy continued. "You know, when I was a kid, I liked two things. Johnny Carson and Westerns. I decided, when I grew up, I was going to rob a bank in every state, get famous." Jimmy gambled on another step forward. "You know how many banks I've robbed?"

"Like, two hundred, something, you said."

The kid turned for approval from the servers, not confident in his answer.

"One," Jimmy said. "Just one. See, when I looked at it, I figured, there's no real money in robbing a bank. It's too difficult. If you carry a gun, you got more chance of being shot. And there's not as much cash in banks as people think, they got sick of being robbed. What I did, I started hitting places like this. Fast businesses, where people paid in cash, and there was no real security. But you know the problem with that?"

There was real doubt in the kid's eyes now, but his finger was still on the trigger, he could pull at any second.

"The problem is, everyone is security now. Walk in a place like this, everyone's got a cell phone, everyone's walking around with surveillance devices. You've just pulled an armed robbery, with no mask, and I'm guessing no getaway plan."

The kid looked round at the other customers now, at the phones they had on the tables in front of them.

Jimmy said, "What you have here is a mistake you made. And you can't un-make it. The cops are gonna come, and you're going to do time. But what you can do is not make an even bigger mistake." Jimmy looked directly at the gun now. "You can put that down."

The gun hand wavered. The eyes behind it, young, confused, really wanted permission to lower the weapon. Jimmy could see it. The anger. The pride. The kid needed to relax.

"What's your name?"

"Uh...Ed."

"What's your full name? Come on, we're all friends here."

"Foley. Ed Foley."

"Ed, you ever hear the one about the three dwarves?"

Ed turned to the servers as if to ask, *is he for real?*

They both shrugged, *don't ask us.*

"See, there are these three dwarves outside the head office for the Guinness Book of Records. Never met each other before, just turned up at the same time. They're asking each other why they're there. I mean, might be the same thing, right? That would be awkward. So the first dwarf says, 'I'm here to get tested. I think I have the smallest hands in the world'. And the other two are like, well...okay. Good luck. It's an achievement, I guess? So he goes in. Thirty minutes later, he comes out. All happy. He's in. Number one. Smallest hands in the world. Awesome. Then the second one says, 'I'm getting tested too. I think I have the smallest feet in the world.' Okay, they say. Well…good luck. He goes in. Thirty minutes later, he comes out. Jumping around, happy. He's in. Smallest feet in the world. Fantastic. So then they ask the third guy. He pauses, he's nervous. He says, 'I'm here to get tested. I think I have the smallest…uh…you know.'" Jimmy made a show of looking down at his crotch. "'I think I have the smallest…*thing*.' And the others, I mean, they want to be supportive, so they go, great, well good luck. So he goes in. Comes out five minutes later. He's all angry, like really shaking. And he looks at them, and he says, 'Who the fuck is Ed Foley?'"

There was a pause. Just long enough for Jimmy to doubt his play. Then Ed started to laugh. One of those that rumbles up, starting like indigestion sounds in the gut, before fighting up the throat. He shook his head and smiled, then laughed again.

He held the gun out, and Jimmy took it.

Sirens were approaching, still a little way off.

Jimmy turned to look over at Megan. "There's your ending."

BARNET FAIR
Inspired by the Rhyming Slang for Hair
Catriona McPherson

Must have been round about two years back it started. I was on a high about the new premises, doing all the promo I could wangle. I didn't even mean to say it that first time. It was only local press, poor cow with her split-ends and her soft shoes stretched over a bunion. She asked about the salon's name and I said what I always say: 'I'm *from* Barnet. Bred and buttered.' Then she goes 'And hairdressers do love a pun, don't they. Like chip shops.'

I saw red then. I was doing her a favour with this interview for her stupid rag. I was entitled to respect. After everything I've been through in my life.

'It's an act of defiance,' I told her. I managed to not to say 'sweetie' at the end. Or 'bitch'.

She perked up at that. Part-time hack on the local birdcage liner and she thinks she's Leonard Bernstein.

'I'm a survivor,' I said. People say that right and left these days. It's lost all its meaning. I half-expected an eye roll from Bunion Bertha when I said it in the interview. But she was gagging for it, as it goes.

'I was assaulted,' I said. 'Sexually assaulted. Gay bashed, actually.'

She was so thrilled to hear *that* little gem she forgot to keep peck-peck-pecking away at her shorthand.

'And that's where it happened,' I said. 'Right there in my hometown. At the fair. So using the name for my salon is a…I don't know what to say. What would you call it?'

'An act of courage?' she suggested. I shrugged it off but I gave her a half-smile and a quarter-nod. She'd use the phrase in the article now, for sure, pleased with herself for hitting the nail. And I didn't look big-headed.

'Do you feel you can share it with the readership?' she asked me. Readership! Bored folk that have finished the mags at the dentist and maybe some house-bound pensioners with the kind of relations that'll give a newspaper subscription for Christmas.

'My memory's hazy,' I told her

'That's well-known, though.'

'And I'd had a few cheeky Vimtos, as it goes. All trolled up for a night on the waltzers, you know?'

'You don't need to apologise for drinking,' she said. 'There are no perfect victims.' Cheeky cow. 'We all know that now. You've got no need to feel guilty.' Oh, she was eating out of my hand.

'This is hard,' I said. 'Talking about it for the first time? It's harder than I thought it would be.'

'The first time?' she said. I swear she had colour in her cheeks from the thrill of it.

'We had met at the burger van,' I said. 'Eyes locked, you know how it goes. And then we went on the big wheel. Very romantic. Stopped at the top. All that.'

'Sounds lovely.' She was turning misty-eyed. Typical hag. Closest she'd ever get to a fit bloke was listening to me describing him.

'Then…I dunno, it gets a bit vague until the bit when we were round the back of something. There was a generator. It could have been one of the rides, or it could have been a living van. I'm not mechanically minded. It's hard to say.'

'And then what happened?' she said. Couldn't have cared less about me setting the scene.

'We kissed. Not a peck, but I don't want to say more. I'm bashful.' I fanned my cheeks and she giggled. 'The next thing I knew, well not really. Like I say, it's hazy. But practically the next thing I knew I'm coming round in the HDU and it's the next morning.'

She shook her head, tutted and waited for more. Her eyes were still shining.

'My mum was there. And one of my aunties. Holding my hand. Asking me what happened. But I wasn't even *out* back then so I said nothing.'

'Didn't the police ask too?'

'They did, yes. And…I'm not proud of this, but…I told them a stranger had lured me away to a dark corner and I ended up with my head bashed in. The looks they gave me, even for *that*! It was different days.'

'And they never caught him?'

'They've never arrested anyone for it,' I said. Which was true.

It's right enough what they say. I got more exposure from telling that hack my sob story than I could have scored from a double-page ad in a national, with full-colour and a coupon. It hit the red-tops and, before you know what's what, the phone's ringing off the hook for more interviews. Then of course they find my wife. Ex-wife. And she's telling the *Mail* I'm straight, so I need to knock that on the head. Bad for business. East, west, bi's best, I always say. My ladies like a bit of camp, but they luurrve a bit of camp with a chance. And so by the time I've done another round of interviews I'm a celebrity. I'm judging talent shows and getting asked to donate auction prizes for a different good cause every bloody day.

Only, with the exposure comes the bleedin' exposure, don't it? My version of that night—all the fun of the fair, I don't think—started to crumble. Next thing, some bloke's come round from the *Guardian Weekend*, asking for my story—full-page, colour photo—and I tried to put the brakes on. He pressed harder. So I thought it over and then I goes: one condition. If I can name the salon and put a link to the website, you are *on*, my son. He give me this funny look, like *he* didn't get *his* wedge.

Thing is, though, the day he arrived on my doorstep with his budget highlights and his mini-recorder, turns out he'd done some homework. 'You weren't the only victim,' he goes. 'Were you?'

'Right, right, right,' I came back with, thinking on my feet. It's always been a talent of mine. 'Ohhhhhh, you've seen that garbled mess that local rag printed up, have you? I was mortified! It made it sound like I was all me me and not a care for the other one.'

I took a drag of my fag, held it and then trickled it out, planning what to say to get him back on my side again. Face on him, just because I was smoking, but it's my salon and we were in my office so he had to lump it. It would have done him a power to take up the sticks himself. Shift a few pounds off him. Anyway, after my bit of thinking time, I carried on. 'Yes,' I said, 'I *did* think I was the target of a trap. At first. That's what I thought when I woke up in the hospital. Course it was, what else? I was out cold, see? Turns out though, that my date—never even knew his name!—was in another ward hooked up to machines in an even worse state than me. Now, why would that bit from the locals lop off half the story like she did? I phoned up and asked but they wouldn't tell me. *You're* a journalist. What was that all about then?'

He shrugged, but I could tell he wanted to defend the honour of the press.

'We do sometimes select a few key facts,' he said. 'And it

can sometimes seem as if the truth's been twisted.'

'But not this time, eh?' I said. 'You'll print my story. My voice. No messing?'

'That's what our readers expect from the column,' he said. 'The straight gen.'

'Well, the straight gen about that night at the fair is this—I pieced it together from what the police were saying when they questioned me—and it wasn't a honey trap set for me at all! Someone who didn't...approve of us kissing slammed into my date and knocked him down on the ground. He bashed his head on the...what do you call it? The thingy that the tow-bar drops onto? Sticking out the back of the trailer? Sticking up? He fell on it. And when he was on the ground...' I stopped.

'What?'

'He got kicked. In the head. In the kidneys. All over.'

'You didn't?'

'Get kicked? Worst that happened to me was my head smashing into the corner of the van. Reinforced, it was. Knocked out cold. I came round in the HDU the next day. Concussion. I couldn't remember a thing. As soon as I was on my feet again, the cops asked and asked and asked. But I couldn't tell them anything. We went round the back of the van, we kissed, I got knocked out, he got done over. I couldn't remember a face or a voice or anything. I said to them to polygraph me but they don't do that in real life,' I said. 'At least not back then. I didn't know that, did you?'

'Did you see him again afterwards?' he asked me. 'The other...boy, I suppose. You were seventeen, weren't you?'

'I never did. I wasn't out. He more'n likely wasn't out. My mum and dad would hardly let me over the door after. They'd never had the police round the house. Never had their names in the papers. I went along with what they said. I just wanted it all to be over.'

'But you're speaking up now,' he goes. 'All these years on.'

'All these years on,' I agreed. I felt a flare of panic, like heartburn, but I ignored it and plastered a smile on. 'My head's up, my shoulders are back. My business is booming. You did say I could mention the salon, didn't you?'

When it came out, Saturday *Guardian* weekend section, I got it mounted and framed, hung it up in reception. Long-time clients who thought they knew me would read it and then look at me with basset eyes.

So business boomed a bit more. I spoke to a Rotary about homophobia. I signed T-shirts for Pride Week and threw them off a low-loader. I got asked to donate to the homeless at Christmas and the refugees at Eid.

When I got the email asking if I'd offer 'something unique' for Cancer Awareness, I deleted it without reading to the end. You can only do so much. I don't know if the sort that had the brass neck to doorstep me at work was the same one that sent it because she never mentioned anything about an email and I could hardly admit to getting it, could I? Just like I could hardly say no when the bint asked me right there at reception in front of Amanda.

'I'd be honoured,' I said. 'Cancer, is it? It's an honour is what it is.'

'A gala dinner and live auction,' she said.

'So…I'd donate like a voucher? Or products?' I was guessing. And I was guessing wrong.

She goes: 'We wondered if you would be willing to offer an experience.' I'm thinking she's a bold one. Never mind that she's marched into an upscale hair salon looking like she cuts her own with a penknife. 'Something more than money could buy,' she's telling me.

'Oo-er,' I said, dropping a hip. But when she didn't laugh I straightened up again and asked her, all business-like: 'What sort of experience were you thinking?'

'Well, hairdressing,' she says. 'We've got The Beaten Olive

Tree kicking in a buffet with wine and we wondered if you'd be willing to do the actual bzzzzzzz. You know—with clippers. Say for six friends? In someone's home?'

'Six haircuts?' I said. 'In someone's front room? I'd rather do it here in the salon. I mean, that's a day's work. Not that I'm not—'

She cut me off. 'Not haircuts,' she said. 'Head shaves. Spread a sheet, plonk a kitchen chair on top and shave heads. For cancer, you know. Solidarity?'

'You think you'll get someone to bid on that? Shouldn't *we* pay *them*?'

'We had a group do it last year. Curry and Clippers, we called it. And if you wanted to, you could always do one of those designs. You know the kind of thing I mean? Can you? They look terribly complicated.'

Patronising mare.

'An undercut?' I said. 'Course, I can. Known for them.'

That's how they get you.

I was as good as signed up to go tripping off to the 'burbs to give intricate razer-dos to a pile of sloppy-drunk book-club mums.

'And I'll take a table at the auction too,' I said, just to wipe the smirk off her face. 'Staff night out for a good cause, eh Amanda?'

I wanted to see who won it, see what I was up against. And by the time I found out how much it cost for a table—two hundred quid a head, if you can wrap your brainbox round it, for a function room in a Best Western!—the staff were too giddy to stand for me changing my mind again. I made damn sure they all had paddles to bid with and told them not to show me up, getting hammered and keeping their hands in their pockets. Because there were salon clients in the room: Mrs. Burns with her bald patch and her bad breath; Julie with the warts on her scalp that was always tutting at me for catching them with my comb till she took herself off and good riddance; Simon Latimer that would never admit he colours his sides grey and his brows black because he reckons he's George Clooney. In his dreams.

They all looked through me like I was a ghost.

'I should have come in a tinting apron and gloves,' I said to Amanda. 'Sparked a memory.'

'Don't be like that,' she said. 'You're too sensitive.'

Typical. She never stops criticizing. If she wasn't cheap, loyal and not averse to a quickie in the supply cupboard I'd sack her for snide digs like that.

'I know,' I said, leaning against her as if she'd said something nice and I was grateful. 'Me and my issues, eh?'

Amanda turned to a waiter passing behind her and asked if that was decaf or real he was carrying. 'Because this lot could do with a pick-me-up, frankly,' she said, pointing at the rest of the staff. 'Free booze and their Spanx too tight to let them eat owt.'

The waiter smirked but said nothing because the auction was starting; the auctioneer up on the podium, rocking on his heels with his thumbs in his braces, waiting for his big moment.

I shushed Amanda. 'They'll start with the tiddlers and work up to the big ones like mine,' I said. That's what the auctioneer had told me, when I met him in the gents between the mains and puddings. He was having a fag and blowing it out the window. I joined him.

'Aaaaaaand first up tonight!' he goes, throwing the mike from hand to hand like a Vegas cabaret, 'Lot No. 1. Laaadies and g'men, we have a luuuurvely little package for you. A buffet supper for six delivered to your home, wine included of course, and a top local hairdresser thrown in to do your Cancer Awareness solidarity head shaves right there on your own livingroom carpet! Slip him a tenner and he'll sweep up the clippings. Won't you, sunshine?'

He winked at me and the roving spot picked me out. So I had to hoist a smile onto my face, as if I wasn't seething. Going first, like I was some kind of warm-up act! Sweeping clippings? I thought we'd bonded over the fag smoke. I was being kind to him, as a matter of fact, sweaty little porker in his braces and his stacked heels trying to look five foot six and failing.

At least the bidding was brisk. It started at two hundred quid and went to four without a pause, three different paddles going up and down like the clappers. Then it slowed and limped to five with just the two of them. At five fifty, the gavel banged and then the winning bidder was coming over to talk dates with me.

He was a standard issue dad on a night out, with bad shoes and a worse shirt—hanging out as if that would hide his belly. And his hair was nothing. He had a bit of a cheek, actually, expecting praise for shaving *that*.

'We did it last year,' he said. 'The same six of us. We shaved our heads and got them tattooed while they were bald. This year we wondered if maybe you could do something fancy. A stubble cancer ribbon or a…'

Tumor, I wanted to say but I bit my lip on it. 'Course I can,' I said instead. 'Anything you fancy. Now then, what night were you thinking?'

It looked good to start with. Nice leafy bit of town and up-lighters on the monobloc drive—serious money.

I recognise the bint that answers the door. She was at the auction, but she's not in her glad rags now: tracky bums and a cut off T-shirt from some half-marathon, with not a lick of make-up. I've made an effort with my high boots and a linen shirt. And she's spared herself the hassle of washing the hair she's shaving off. Her scalp grease is going to choke my clippers if I'm not lucky.

'You have a lovely home,' I say to her.

She wrinkles her nose at me. 'It's not my house,' she goes.

'Where are we setting up? I've got a sheet to put down on

the carpet.'

'Oh there's no carpet.' She's showing off, even though she's just said it's not hers. As if a carpet's as naff as ruffle blinds and she's laughing at me.

As I follow her through to a lounge that opens right off the entrance hall with just a swoop of wall to stop the drafts, no door, I see that a carpet *would* look a bit out of place. The floor's polished concrete like a wine bar and the furniture—what there is—is grey suede. There's some plug ugly art too. The worst of the paintings is six feet square if it's an inch, black and grey slashes and not even framed, but there's a light trained on it as if it's the Mona Lisa.

I spot the rest of them round another swoop of wall, standing in the kitchen, they're all looking down at something I can't see over the breakfast bar. Or maybe not a breakfast bar. Maybe I'd get another nose wrinkle for calling it that. They're in a circle, staring downwards, and their faces are sombre, the five of them. Three men and another two women, all of them in T-shirts, none of them in jewelry. I'm fuming. This was supposed to be a smart night.

They're on the move, now, coming towards me.

'Welcome, welcome,' goes the first man to see me. It must be *his* house. He's got that look about him—huge watch, boat shoes, proper salt and pepper Clooney-do, like he's never had to count a penny in his life. I can't work out which one of the women he's married to. None of them are arm-candy, that's for damn sure. He calls back over his shoulder. 'Where should the guest of honour put his coat?' Not the owner then. He turns back to me. 'Or are you keeping it on?'

Before I can answer, I hear a scurry of feet overhead and then thumps as—it sounds like—a herd of baby elephants comes hammering down the stairs. It's two kids, teenagers. They go coiling round the adults like cats, to get to the kitchen. They're loading plates with free food that the caterers dropped off.

'Go easy,' says another of the men. He's as thin as a whippet with Dracula hair brushed back and gelled stiff, long thin sideburns like stilettoes. He doesn't look like a dad—he looks as gay as poodle in leg warmers, if I'm honest—nor like the owner of this place neither. 'Don't eat all the prawns.'

The kids are looking down too now, laughing. Then, balancing plates and hugging bottles of pop under their arms, they scamper off upstairs again. From the kitchen comes a whirring noise I can't place. Dishwasher? Freezer? But it's getting closer and round the swoop of wall comes an electric wheelchair. In it, there's a little gnome of a man all curled down, neck arched, the knobs of his spine sticking out like knuckles, chin on his chest.

He's got a kind of a clicker in one hand and, as I watch, a string of letters starts marching over a screen off to one side of him. *Hello Marty*, it says. *Nice to see you.*

'Nice to meet you too,' I say.

'Marty?' says the woman who let me in and laughed about carpets. 'Don't look at the screen. He prefers it if you look him in the eye.'

'Of course,' I say. Stupid bitch. The way he's crunched over? To look him square in the boat I'd have had to crouch in front of his wheelchair and peer upwards. And I don't fancy it, seeing as how he's wearing a bib and it's soaked through. Poor sod. Lucky sod as well, mind you, with all these pals making sure he got included in the evening. Cheeky sods *they* are, dragging a raspberry ripple along. It was supposed to be an elegant gathering, what with the donated champagne and finger food. Quail eggs and lychees those kids had, as well as the prawns.

And now bloody Stephen Hawking's sat in the middle with his bib and his knee-blanket. I wouldn't have offered this experience if I'd known there were special needs involved. Not that I'm cruel; just that I've got my own issues. I'm easily upset.

'Right then,' I go, turning away. It's not as if you could

have a conversation with him. 'Shall we eat, drink and be merry first? Or shave the old bonces and drown the sorrows after?'

'I don't know about anyone else,' says the third man. It's the dad who came over after the bidding, but he wasn't hiding a belly, as it goes. Stripped to a basketball jersey and long shorts, he looks a bit of a gym-hound. 'But I'd rather you didn't have any champers till you're done with the razor. No offence.'

'And there won't be sorrow,' says the woman who's standing with her hand in his back pocket. It's the one who came into the salon to press-gang me. Yoga-type. Barefoot tonight, even at a drinks do. 'We did it last year,' she goes. 'I thought you knew. So we're ready for what we look like.'

'And you were thinking of undercuts?' I say. I'm taking charge now, tired of them pissing me about. I open my case and spread the dust sheet down on the polished concrete. 'Might take a bit longer but I'm more than happy.'

'We changed our mind,' says the third woman. She's younger than the rest, but not scared to speak for them. Maybe it's *her* house. 'We did something a bit extra last year but this year we're just going to get them shaved and see what happens.'

Whatever that means.

She goes first. Once she's slipped off her do-rag, I carve the length off with my long shears. Not much length, as it goes, seeing it's only a year since the last shaving. Then I put the zero on my clippers and bend her head forward. She's got some kind of birthmark on her skull, I notice—or think I notice—as the overhead light hits. I take the clippers up from her nape—nice hairline; I could have done a spider's web undercut if she'd let me—and run it right over to her brow, a spill of hair falling away on either side like snow from a plough. I love to watch it. Never gets old.

That's some weird birthmark, I think, as I glance back at her scalp. It's a ring shape. Hollow. I take the clippers back to her nape and shave off another strip. It's got a straight bit, the birthmark. And it's not a birthmark at all. It's a tattoo!

'We did it last year,' says the man with stiletto sideburns. 'We've all got one.'

I've uncovered the whole thing now. It's an R.

'You...all got your initials tattooed on your heads?' I say.

'Nope,' says the woman I'm shaving. Then before I can think what to say to that she goes on. 'Have *you* got any ink, Marty?'

'Not me,' I tell her. 'I'm bad with needles after everything I've been through.'

I wait.

'Me too,' goes the big guy with the watch. 'So the back of my head was the perfect spot. I couldn't see a damn thing.'

Suddenly, they all go quiet and the room's silent except for a low beeping noise I can't place at first. Then I notice where they're all looking and realise it's the wheelchair guy clicking words out onto his screen and the rest of them just sitting like pillocks watching them.

'Toto's asking what gave you the needle phobia,' says Gym Dad, reading it.

'Toto?' I ask.

'Nickname,' says the yoga woman.

'I've got quite a few issues,' I say. 'PTSD, I suppose is the best thing to call it for quick.'

'Ohhhhhh,' said Watch Man. 'From the...incident? Who was it said they'd read about it.'

Then they all stop speaking again while 'Toto' beep-beeps another message. It would drive me nuts if I had to put up with him every day, but maybe they've only brought him along for a special treat. Maybe one of this lot is his carrier.

'Toto read about it,' says the woman I'm shaving. Have finished shaving actually. I let her smell both kinds of lotion I've brought with me, the citrus one and the rose. She goes for rose and I smooth it onto her scalp, trying not to wonder what the great big R stands for, if it's not her initial.

'A gay-bashing?' says Watch Man, reading the screen and then lifting his eyes to me. 'That's horrific.'

'You next?' I say.

He takes half a step back, his face falling, before he realises I mean for a shave. Then he swallows and steps forward to the seat, while I'm brushing the first woman's hair off the stool and cleaning my clippers.

He's quicker than her because he's kept his short all year. I can see the tattoo through the growth even before I start, because I know it's there and I'm looking. It's a T, I see, as his scalp is revealed.

'But not your initial?' I say.

'Not my initial,' he echoes. 'I'll take the citrus, by the way.'

'Toto's asking if they ever caught the people who did it,' the oily scalp woman pipes up. I didn't hear the beeping, used to it already. Maybe that's how they can stand him hanging round their parties: because he fades into the background. Mind you, Yummy Yoga's changing his bib. That would stay pretty sickening. She rolls it up and drops it on the floor, reaching round him to put on a fresh one.

'They never did,' I say. 'I never saw anyone. I couldn't describe anyone.'

'What about the other guy?' asks Gym Dad. 'There *was* another guy, wasn't there? You were together? That's how they knew you were gay?'

'Bi,' I say, like I always do. 'The forgotten letter in the bowl of alphabet soup.'

'Right, right,' Gym Dad says. He's taking the shoulder gown from Watch Man and sitting in the chair.

'And the other guy?' says Olyve Oyl, with the scalp.

'He was even worse off than me,' I say. 'My head got slammed into a metal support and it knocked me out. I was in hospital with concussion. But the other guy—'

'Your boyfriend?' says Dracula, with the stiletto sideburns.

'Date, wasn't it?' says Yummy Yoga.

'Not even that,' I tell her. 'A hook-up. We'd only met minutes before. In fact, I didn't even know what he was about, at first. At first, I thought—'

But I stop myself before I say it, not knowing how it would go down with this lot.

Toto's beeping again. Yummy Yoga slews to the side to read what he's got to say.

'Behave!' she goes, when he's finished. 'I'm not saying that.'

'You can't offend me,' I tell her. 'It's shit off a shovel to me, love. Life I've led. Things I've seen.'

I'm shaving Gym Dad now. I start in the middle, dying to see what letter's tattooed on him. N, it turns out to be.

'And it's not your initial?' I say.

'It's not my initial,' he says.

'What did he write?' I say, looking at the Yummy Yoga.

She frowns. 'You can talk to Toto, Marty.'

'Sorry,' I say. 'I'm slow learner.' I freeze after it's out, thinking no way I should say 'slow learner' in front of an actual drooling cretin, but they don't seem to mind. I glance at Toto and notice for the first time that he's got a little mirror arrangement set up on the other arm of his chair from the screen. It's on a bendable stalk, like an angle-poise lamp. If I look at it I can see his face reflected there and he can see me too. 'What did you say?' I ask him, feeling a right plonker, seeing he can't answer, except in beeps.

'He said he bets you thought it was a drug deal,' says Yummy. 'At first. Not a hook up.'

I swallow. 'As it goes. That's a pretty good guess. I mean, not a 'drug deal'. A bit of blow for a Friday night. Nothing nasty.'

'And what did you say happened to him?' says the young one, with the R. 'The other guy. The drug dealer.'

'He wasn't!' I tell her. 'He was as keen as me to hook up. It could have been a magical night if the 'phobe hadn't seen us going round the back of the van and followed us.'

'Lucky,' says Watch Man. 'He lures you round the back of a van at a fun fair. You think he's got a bit of blow to sell. Then he makes his move and it turns out you're gay. Could have ended badly for him otherwise.'

'Bi,' I say. I've finished Mr. N without hardly noticing what I'm doing and now I'm rubbing rose lotion over his scalp, without asking. 'It *did* end badly. He got kicked in the head. Steel-toe cap boots. He needed surgery.

Olyve Oyl sucks her teeth. 'Terrible,' she says. 'What was his name?'

'I never asked,' I said. 'Like I was telling you. It was a hook-up.'

'But afterwards.' She's coming over to sit in the chair now, ready to gunk up my good clippers. 'You must have read the newspaper reports, didn't you?'

'My mum tried to protect me,' I said, which was true. 'And the papers always called him by his surname…I can't remember it now. A long time ago and all the trauma.'

'I can imagine,' she says. 'It sounds absolutely terrifying, what you went through.'

'It was,' I agree. 'Thank you for understanding.' But the silence in the room's a surprise. I'd expected a ripple of sympathy from the rest of them. They're like statues. Especially the bald ones. Sitting stone-face and shiny, staring at me.

I look back down to the scalp I'm uncovering. Her skin's dark and the tat doesn't show up well but the light's good and I can tell it's an E.

'E,' I say. 'Is it code for something?' I'm still thinking about drugs. About that guess that was far too lucky.

Beep, beep, beep. And then Stiletto Sideburns says: 'Toto's giving you a clue.' I wait. 'R, A, N, E. And two of us to go.'

'Oh my God!' I say, as the penny drops. 'You've never all got CANCER spelled out across your bonces, have you? That's…'

'Of course not,' says Sideburns. 'That would be beyond morbid. And what good would it do?'

'And they're in that order, are they?' I say.

'Nope,' says Watch Man. 'We can't make it too easy for you.'

'So you're not a C,' I say to Yummy Yoga, as she sits down and pulls the cape around herself.

'I'm not a C,' she says. 'Get cracking and see for yourself.'

There's no chatter now. There's no sound at all except the hum of my clippers and the shush of hair falling over the nylon cape and dropping like snowflakes onto the dust sheet.

It's a T I uncover on her bony, white skull.

'TRANE,' I say. 'TARNE. I'm not good at these…what do you call them?'

'Anagrams,' says Sideburns. 'Listen, before you do me. Can you check out Toto. Could you have a feel of his scalp and see if you'd be happy to shave it? I know we said six and that would make it seven but maybe you'd stretch a point?'

'Course,' I say, even though there's sweat popping out on my palms at the thought of touching that curled-down head on its crooked neck.

At least when I stand behind him I can read what he's tapping out on his screen without anyone needing to relay it to me.

Not sure I'd suit a Picard job, he writes.

'For a good cause though,' I say. But truth is, I've never felt anything like the mess of his scalp under his pelt of hair. My fingers probe and stroke and I can't tell *what* I'm touching.

'I've got a lot of lumps and bumps up there.

'I feel them. What are they? Not…I mean, I hope they're not. I mean…what with this being a cancer charity thing…'

Not tumors. Scars. From surgery.

'Ohhhhh. Did you sue your surgeon?'

No one laughs.

I wasn't always this way. It was brain damage. It happened when I was twenty.

I take my hands off his head as if they're burning. I stare at the screen.

It was a gay bashing.

I take a step back. But there's someone right behind me, stopping me moving farther away.

I'm not bi, he writes. *Let me rephrase that. I'm no more bi than you are, Marty. But it was a smart move. I'll give you that. It was a stroke of genius.*

'What?' I say, but no one believes me. I don't even sound convincing to myself.

They never caught the guy, he writes. *So I put it behind me. Got my degree. Started my business. Met my husband. Bought this house. Adopted our children. I've got a good life. And great friends. It would never have crossed my mind again if you hadn't decided to start speaking.*

I unstick my tongue form the roof of my mouth and try to run it round my gums. It catches. When I open my lips there's a clicking sound, loud as his letters. 'What did I say? What did I—' I manage not to let the words 'get wrong' slip out of me.

We never went on the big wheel. We never locked eyes. I wondered why you'd say that if it wasn't true. Then it struck me. It was supposed to convince the cops and your mum that you were a victim too.

I feel my face go pale and there's a sinking lump in my guts. I really did say that, didn't I? About the big wheel and the looks of lust. I made a sweet puppy-love story to make myself feel better and all these years later when I started talking to that local hag, that was the tale that came out. I'd nearly forgotten it wasn't true.

I open my mouth with another click. 'What are you going to do to me?' I say.

'We haven't decided,' says Stiletto Sideburns. That's who's standing behind me. 'Toto's a much nicer man than I am, aren't you darling? I'd string you up. But all he wanted was a chance to look you in the eye and hear your side.'

'There was no one else there.' I can't get the words out my mouth quick enough. 'I thought he was selling. He made a pass. I panicked. I shoved him. And when he was down. I kicked him.'

'Who are you talking to, Marty?' says Yummy Yoga. 'Who's 'he'?'

'You!' I say. I look in the mirror, at his eyes staring back into mine. 'I kicked you. I forgot what I was wearing. I forgot I'd come straight from work. On a building site. Steel toe caps. And then, when I saw what I'd done…'

You nutted the metal bar and knocked yourself out.

I nod.

And then you lied and lied and lied and lied and lied and lied. He must have a shortcut key the speed the words are spilling onto his screen. He's shaking, spit flying out of both corners of his mouth from the way his breath is heaving in and out.

'Toto, don't upset yourself,' his husband says. 'The kids are upstairs. They might come down. Don't let them see you like this.'

And lied and lied and lied and lied and lied.

'I lied,' I say, to stop those words jerking out onto the screen. 'I had to 'come out' to keep the story going. So I said I was bi. I married a woman. I do wome—sleep with women. But I say I'm bi and who's going to argue? I'm a hairdresser, for God's sake. No one bats an eye.' I can feel the tears starting. I don't want to show myself up, dissolving in front of this crowd of sadists. But I can't help it. 'What are you going to *do* with me?'

We're going to sentence you to the worst punishment you can imagine.

My mouth's not dry now. It's flooding, as my stomach heaves.

'It was Toto's idea,' says Olyve Oyl. 'I'm his lawyer and I advised him against it. So did his husband, his trainer.' She's pointing at them all. 'His PA, his best friend and *her* husband. We all think he should call the police, but it's Toto's decision.'

And I choose this for you, Marty. You're going to live your empty life, telling your lies, acting out your cover story. All I ask is that you put a photograph up in your salon. Big as you can blow it up. You in the middle and the six of my dear friends ranged on either side, facing backwards, spelling out the thing you'll never forget. We've got a good camera. One of the kids will take the picture.

'You can't get children involved in this!' I say.

'They'll never know,' says Watch Man. 'It'll look like a joke. Like a charity stunt. Hell, it'll look like a good advert for your business. We're going to send it to the papers. See if we can get coverage. It'll be in all the cancer awareness campaigns for sure.'

'Yes, Marty,' says Stiletto Sideburns. He's loving it. 'This picture's going to pop up every time anyone Googles you for the rest of your days. You just need to shave me and we're good to go.'

'Come on then,' I say, through numb lips. My guts are still churning. The coldness of them. The deviousness it took to set this up, last year for the tatts and this year to reel me in. 'Let's get cracking, Mr. B.'

The smile he gives me would freeze the warts off a toad, burn the hide off a rhino.

I step back onto the dustsheet and start up the clippers, as he turns his back and offers his head to me.

TEA LEAF
Inspired by the Rhyming Slang for Thief
Susanna Calkins

Maria's text is stark and, quite frankly, irritating. "Hurry up," it says.

Even though I don't want to, I still find myself picking up my pace as I walk towards Second Street. Maria is my boss after all. But after months of working late nights at a bar, my body finds it hard to adjust to the morning hours required of my new job as a jewelry store clerk. And of course, there had been Dmitri. I hadn't seen him in several weeks, so we'd enjoyed getting reacquainted last night.

My face cracks into a wide grin as I think about how he'd woken me with a kiss earlier. *Dana, I gotta go,* he'd whispered, his deep blue eyes peering into my own. *But I have a surprise for you tonight. The start of something new. I'll give it to you, before your shift at the bar.*

He'd left before I had a chance to tell him that I'd been fired from that bar. That I'd started a new job in the weeks he'd been away. Oh, well. There was time. I'd tell him later.

When I step into Jenkins Diamonds, the bell jangles over my head in its irritating way. Maria, a petite Latina dressed in her customary dark blue suit, glares at me. "Dana, you're late," she says, pointing rather dramatically to her watch. "I expected you here fifteen minutes ago."

Fifteen minutes late doesn't seem so bad to me, but I bite back a retort as self-preservation kicks in. I really can't afford to lose another job, and Maria knows that. I have debts, bills to pay, and unfortunately, I like nice things, which means I really need to stay employed. Besides, she hired me despite the fact that I had no background in retail, so I just give her an apologetic smile. "Sorry," I say. "It won't happen again."

"I have a big client meeting later," she says, touching her sleek black hair. Apparently mollified by my contriteness. "Off-site."

I shrug, not as impressed as I'm sure she'd like. Her big client was probably some rich North Shore woman seeking to pawn her cast-off jewelry to maintain appearances. I'd learned early on that's what most of those "client meetings" entailed. We were really nothing more than a high-toned pawn shop, tricked out in a veneer of wealth and glamour, with our sparkly carpet and dazzling displays.

Sighing, I go behind the long counter, reaching for the rag and blue glass cleaner which were always stored in convenient reach. I begin to wipe the glass top of the showcase, removing the non-existent fingerprints and grime from the glass. The owner, Mr. Jenkins, was kind of fanatical about fingerprints, I'd learned. Like a few fingerprints would really keep someone from buying a diamond bracelet.

As I move the cloth in indifferent circles along the glass, Maria comes over and unlocks the large sliding doors behind the long counter. Since not everything will fit in the display cases, the extra stock is stored in rows of individually locked storage trays stacked in drawers beneath the case.

"Inventory time," she says, handing me a stack of printed pages stapled at the corner and a set of little keys that fit each tray. "Just compare the items in all trays in each drawer against the stock list. Start on the bottom row."

Taking the list, I crouch down behind the counter. As I insert the key into the bottom drawer, I am startled to discover that it's already unlocked.

That's not good. When I had first started the job, I was told repeatedly that all drawers must be relocked after trays are taken out to show a customer. Forgetting to re-lock a drawer was a firing offense.

I stifle a groan when I realize this drawer is the one that contains trays of sparkling tennis bracelets. I remember removing a tray the day before, to show the bracelets to some hippy chic retro-wannabes. Ugh. I'd probably forgotten to lock the drawer when I was done.

I glance at the rotating camera swiveling around the room, and then I pretend to unlock the drawer. Saying a slight prayer to a god I'm not even sure about, I pull the top tray out. Thankfully, all twelve tennis bracelets still gleam on their plush purple cushion, as do those in the tray below. A careful check against the printout shows that each bracelet is present and accounted for. Hopefully no one will ever know about my mistake.

But then, when I try the next drawer, I discover that it too is unlocked. This one is full of men's Rolexes, and I don't remember showing any the day before. I frown, glancing at the camera again. Once again, I pretend to unlock the tray before pulling it open.

A quick survey of the contents of the tray shows me that nothing is missing in this drawer either. Still, it's strange. I weigh calling Maria over to tell her, but I squash the idea. *Why borrow trouble,* I remember an old lady shaking her finger at me once. For the first time, I understand what that old lady had meant.

As I move on to the third drawer, which contains Lady Date Just Rolexes for women, the bell above the entrance rings again.

I expect to hear Maria's chirpy greeting, gushing over the early morning customer in her own particular way.

Instead, I hear a sharp intake of breath. *"¡Dios!"* she says in Spanish, her voice unexpectedly strained and hoarse. "What are you doing?!"

Without thinking, I stand up quickly, causing blood to rush forcefully to my head. For a moment, I am too dizzy to focus and I shut my eyes.

Then, when I open my eyes again, I cannot make sense of what I am seeing. Maria is facing me, her face expressing intense fear and shock.

A man in all black stands between us, his back to me, a hoodie pulled over his head.

Two thoughts surge into my mind. *Robber. Gun.*

And then, a question tears at my heart. *Will this be the day I die?*

An icy shock runs over me, and my knees start to buckle. Across the room, Maria's terrified eyes meet mine.

The man tosses an olive messenger bag to Maria. "Fill this up," he says. "Be quick about it."

I inhale sharply. That voice! It couldn't be!

"Dana, run!" Maria cries.

Hearing her words, the man whirls around and stares at me.

I take him in, his stance, his size. And through the mask, deep-ringed blue eyes. Eyes that I had just looked into this morning. My boyfriend's eyes. Dmitri.

For a long moment, we stare at each other. I see him take in my dressy top, read my nametag. Dana Miller, Sales Associate. Only when Maria begins to sob does he break the intense silence.

"Bitch!" he says, turning away from me.

At the ugly word, my throat closes up and I stumble back against the wall, trying to keep from falling. "Oh my God," I hear myself say, distantly through the great rushing in my ears.

The man—Dmitri!—begins to pace. Then he glares at Maria. "I didn't tell you to stop," He nods to where I was standing, without looking at me again. "Now those cases. With the watches."

Maria crosses the room and hands me the bag, her hands trembling. "Please, Dana," she says. "Do as he says."

I take the strap. "He won't hurt us," I whisper to her, before starting to empty the watches into the bag. I say it more to myself, than to her, but her eyes widen.

"How do you know?" she asks.

I shake my head and continue to fill the bag, my fingers clumsy and numb from fear. I am trying desperately to make sense of what is happening.

"Dana," she says, more loudly this time. "How do you know he won't hurt us? Why do you say that?"

"Enough talking!" Dmitri snaps. He cracks his neck. I know his anger is growing. I've seen his before. Once when he was angry at our upstairs neighbor for playing music too loud. Another time when he wasn't satisfied with his cell operator's customer service. This is worse though. He needs to calm down.

"Please," I whisper, transfixed by his waving gun. "Don't!"

"You wanted a witness? Is that it?" He turns back to Maria. "Well, we don't need *you!*"

Then with that, he shoots Maria, before turning to look back at me. Is there a pleading look in his eyes? I can't say for sure.

Senseless, I can only clap my hand over my mouth as I stare at the blood flowing from Maria's head, onto the sparkly gray carpeted floor. It's hard to make sense of what I'm seeing.

"Oh hell." He looks down at Maria, before turning back to me. He leans over the counter and I hand him the bag with the jewelry and watches. He sees me shaking. "Just keep your mouth shut and it'll be alright."

Did he wink then? I'm not sure.

He unlocks the front door and walks out onto the street. When the door shuts, the bell jangles above.

I crawl over to Maria, whose eyes are fluttering. "I'm so sorry Maria," I say beginning to cry. I take her hand. "I didn't know he would shoot you."

Her eyes are confused, terrified, and already clouding over. She whispers something then, which I can't quite catch. I think it was in Spanish. Then she takes two last great breaths, and her chest stops rising at all.

It takes everything I have to lay my ear near her chest.

She is dead.

I don't know how long I've been kneeling beside Maria's body. But dimly I hear the bell when it jangles again. I begin to crawl away, fearful that Dmitri would return. Should I hide? Where should I go? My legs aren't working right at all. Now they are made of jelly. Wobbling jelly. I begin to laugh to myself as I imagine my knees as jelly. Better than thinking about Maria's brains as jelly.

"Excuse me?" A man calls out, his voice oddly cheerful. "Anyone here? I'm looking to get a gift for—" Then, "What the hell?"

I just stare at him. I manage to say some words but they sound muddied, distant, as if I am lying in the deepest dregs of a swamp.

The man had pulled out his cell phone. "Hang on. I'm calling 9-1-1."

I sit back then, unable to look away from Maria's still form.

More time passes, but I don't know how much. Someone throws a blanket around my shoulders.

"She's in shock," I hear someone say.

Someone else tries to put something hot into my hands, but I cannot unlock my arms from around my knees. I need something to hang on to, something to keep me upright in this low staggering nightmare.

"Miss, can you tell us what happened here?" someone asks, crouching down beside me. Places her hand on my shoulder and shakes me. Evidently reads my nametag. Speaks more forcefully. "Dana! Who did this? Was this a burglary? Did you see where the burglars went?"

I latch onto just one of the questions. *Who did this?* Dmitri's eyes looking back into mine. That wasn't the Dmitri I knew. I shake my head. I didn't know that man. I don't know where he went or what he's doing.

"I don't know anything," I murmur. "I mean, yes. It was a burglary. I don't know where he went."

"He?" The police seize on the gender. "A man? Just one man? Can you describe him?"

"He wore a mask. Please," I plead. "I need to call my boyfriend, Dmitri. I need to speak with him."

"We can call him," one of the uniformed officers says. "But first we need to take you to the hospital. You've had quite a shock."

When another officer enters the store, they turn their attention from me. I hear muffled bits of conversation. "Jenkins is on his way. He'll pull up the security footage."

I stand up, still clutching the blanket around me, and move toward the door. I want to be away from the cops looking behind the counters. Away from the photographer snapping pictures of the store. Away from the body.

Avoiding eye contact, I slip out the door, that infernal bell jangling as I step onto the street. Every movement is labored. Everything around me seems in slow motion. One thought overrides everything now. *Must find Dmitri.* I hope I didn't say it out loud.

I can't shake the image of Dmitri shooting Maria, of the

blood seeping from her wound. Of her life ebbing away. I make it halfway down the street before I begin to vomit.

"Are you all right?" a passer-by asks me.

I shake my head, and the gesture worsens my nausea. I lose my balance, and the ground swarms up to meet me.

I wake up at the hospital, an IV line in my arm. I feel my forehead, touching the bandage that someone has wrapped around the sore spot.

"Just a minor concussion," the nurse says to me, having noticed my eyes were open. She continues to check my vitals. "We're giving you something for the pain. And we'll have to hold you overnight for observation. Is there someone I can call for you?"

"Dmitri, my boyfriend," I gasp. Then, the events of the morning wash over me. "Although, maybe not. I mean, he might be away."

"Away?"

"He might have taken a trip. I'm having trouble remembering."

"That's to be understood. Concussions can cause short-term memory loss." Her tone offers a studied professional comfort. "You'll remember. How about your parents? Or a friend?"

No, no, there's no one. My parents died when I was a teenager, and I really didn't have any friends. "I'll be fine," I say. Dmitri had been my friend, these last few months. My other friends had slipped away, and I don't even know how it had happened.

"Some detectives have been waiting to speak to you," she says. "I'll bring them in."

A man and a woman step into my hospital room, and flash me their badges. The male detective introduces himself as Detective Wilson. He looms over his partner, Detective Lee. They both wear rumpled suits and serious shoes, just like detectives do on TV. Their demeanor is friendly and solicitous but their smiles don't reach their eyes when they shake my hand. They inquire after my health, and then begin to ask the same questions I remember answering earlier. *Could I describe the burglar? Had he been alone? Which direction had he gone? Was he on foot?*

Then the bombshell question. "Did you know him?"

A stabbing pain seared through my forehead. "Did I know him?" That murdering thief was not my Dmitri. Not the friend who'd held my hand when we'd had to put my dog to sleep. Not the man who'd made me laugh when I was down about my family. Not the man I'd shared a bed with. "No, of course I didn't know him."

In the morning, when I am released from the hospital, I find Detective Wilson waiting for me.

"We have a few more questions for you," he says. "It would be best if we could talk down at the station. Just a few things we were hoping you could clear up."

"I'm hungry," I mutter. Besides I needed to know if Dmitri was back at our apartment. I just had to speak to him. "Can't this wait?"

"How about I buy you a donut on the way."

The donut turns out to be a stale mistake. One bite and I'm retching into a police station wastebasket. With a grimace, Detective Wilson puts the trashcan out in the hallway no doubt to keep the smells at bay. Detective Lee joins us, and leads me into a small room with three chairs and a table. Is this an interrogation room? Am I being interrogated?

Though I want to bolt out of the room, I plop down into one of the chairs and put my head in my hands.

"You're not well," Detective Lee sounding almost kind.

"Concussion," I say, tapping my head.

The detectives nod knowingly. I can tell they are searching my face, looking for something. What? What are they looking for?

I see them glance at each other.

"How about I get you some water," Detective Wilson says, about to exit the room.

"I'll take tea if you have it," I call. Anything to stall.

Detective Lee smiles. "You're in luck. I just brewed some. I do real tea, leaves and all. Stay here. I'll be right back."

For a moment, I am left alone. There is a mirror. Are they on the other side, watching me?

I don't have to wait long. Detective Lee returns just a moment later, placing a Styrofoam cup in front of me.

"I don't use an infuser," she says, sounding oddly apologetic. "Just wait until the leaves drop to the bottom and then it'll be ready to drink."

"And then you'll read my fortune?" I say, staring down at the steaming drink. *What would mine say? You've been sleeping with a thief?* I am lost until the detective brings me back.

"If you like," she says. "Or you can just tell us the truth. It will be much easier to predict your fortune if you stop lying to us." Her tone has lost all warmth.

"L-Lying to you?" I stammer. All of this has to be a mistake. Later, Dmitri and I will snuggle on the sofa, and he'd be there to comfort me, saying how odd it was that the thief had resembled him. And we'd mourn Maria together, and hurl invectives at the sorry sot who had stolen her life. But the detectives have other ideas.

Detective Wilson enters the room then, pushing a cart with a TV and combined VCR-DVD player. He plugs the equipment in and stays by the door. Looms.

"Tell us. When did you start working at the jewelry store?" Detective Lee asks.

"Oh just a few weeks ago," I say.

"We've checked your employment history," she continues. "You've mostly worked in the food industry, isn't that right? Bars, restaurants, that sort of thing?"

"I worked in retail when I was in college," I say.

"Before you dropped out of college, you mean," Detective Wilson says.

I glare at him.

"So how come Ms. Garcia hired you?" he probes. "Why you? You lack relevant experience."

I shrug. "I guess she thought I'd do a good job." But even to my own ears that sounds lame. Truth was, I'd wondered about it myself. Why had Maria hired me?

My last night at the bar came back to me. *Me, yelling at a handsy customer. My manager, siding with the disgusting fat man who had groped me. Getting fired. At least the bartender had poured me a farewell drink. It was then that Maria Garcia had approached me. 'What an asshole," she had said. "So you're outta here now."*

"Yeah," I'd mumbled. "Now I gotta find another job. Rent's due."

"You know I've seen you here before. You do good work. Ever work in retail?"

"Not really."

Then one thing led to another and before I knew it I'd found myself hired at Jenkins' Diamonds, where I'd been working for the last two weeks. Maria had been fairly patient with me, but I'd also worked reasonably hard, not wanting to shoot my shiny gift horse in the mouth.

"We've got the security footage from the robbery," Detective Wilson says, turning on the TV set. A familiar image of Jenkins' Diamonds appears on the screen. "We'd like you to talk us through it."

I can feel sweat beading on my forehead. The thought of Dmitri. Of Maria. The blood. Bile rises in my throat, threatening to gag me. "Oh, is that necessary?" I ask, trying to appear unruffled.

"Oh yes. We have some questions." He presses 'play.'

I find myself leaning closer, trying to make sense of it. He had started the footage earlier than I expect, before the robbery. Only Maria could be seen. She is doing what I imagine were the usual morning things, shutting off the alarm, opening the security windows, moving chairs into place.

We watch as she checks her watch several times, and peers out the front window. She moves into the middle of the room, where she is in full sight of all security cameras. She is tapping her feet. "Where is she?" we can hear her say. "Why is she late?" We watch her text someone on her phone, frowning the whole while.

Detective Wilson pauses the image. "She's waiting for you, isn't she? We pulled her phone records. We know she's texting you."

My blood begins to race again, remembering how I'd spent my morning. "Yes. I was late."

He resumes play and then after a few minutes, there is footage of me entering the store, looking a bit frazzled and annoyed. We hear her berate me and then we see me give her the finger behind when she turns away. I had forgotten about that and guilt washes over me.

Detective Lee glances at me, but doesn't say anything. We continue to watch. Now, there's footage of me opening up the glass cases and drawers. I watch myself find the open drawers and glance up at the camera and then back to the drawer. My stomach clenches.

This time Detective Lee pauses the image. "What's happening here?" she asks.

"The drawers were unlocked," I explain. "I found them that way."

"Why didn't you say anything to your boss? That seems odd."

"I thought I had forgotten to lock them the night before."

"Do you often forget to lock the cases?"

The blood rushes up in my face. "No, I've never forgotten."

"So all the cases were unlocked, but you were pretending to unlock them. Got it. Let's move on."

Shortly after, Dmitri walks in with the mask drawn over his face. He locks the door behind him, and waves towards Maria. At the sound of his voice, we can see me poke my head up, and him turn towards me. I strain again to see his features, but they were completely obscured.

We watch as Maria comes over and hands me the bag. "Fill it, Dana." Her voice is softer than I remember, more pleading here.

Together we watch as I fill the bag with watches and bracelets, and then we hear me say something to her.

"You spoke softly, but we had a lip reader read your words. '*He won't hurt us,*' you told her. Why would you say that to her?"

I don't answer because I am transfixed by the next section of the video. Even though I know what would happen next, I can't look away. Dmitri comes over to us then. I try to remember his expression. Shocked? Angry? Maybe a bit sad. *"You wanted a witness, is that it?"* he asks and then turns and shoots Maria in the head.

I put my face in my hands. Tears threaten but I strive to contain myself. He must have planned the theft with Maria. Maybe she had told him that the store would be empty. That she would be alone. Why had she wanted a witness then? To have someone who could report on her innocence?

I think about the unlocked shelves, her insistence that I be there, her concern when I was late. Maybe she needed me there because she knew the cops would figure out it was an inside job.

Had Dmitri known? No, not possible. He'd been furious I was there. That's why he shot her, I just know it. But perhaps *she* had known that Dmitri was my boyfriend. In fact, hadn't

I shown her a picture of Dmitri on my phone?

Things began to click then. She'd wanted to frame me. And she had double-crossed him that much was clear. A wave of anger washes over me.

I catch Detective Lee watching me. Who knew what expressions I'd just conveyed?

"Was Ms. Garcia not supposed to be there?" she asks.

"What do you mean?" I ask, jolting upright.

"The perp's clearly talking to *you* here. That comment about witnesses."

"No! He was talking to *her!* She must have been in on it. That's why the cases were unlocked. She was trying to frame me. I see that now."

Neither detective looks like they believe me.

"Then perhaps you can explain what he says here," Detective Wilson says. "'*Just keep your mouth shut and you'll be all right.*'"

But I wasn't all right, was I Dmitri? I stare at the man who was my boyfriend, captured on the small screen, willing him to explain what he had just done.

"What about what you say here?" the detective says, interrupting my thoughts. We all watch as I sink beside my boss's body. *"I'm so sorry, Maria,"* we hear me say. *"I didn't know he would shoot you."*

The words damn me. Still I try to explain. "I wasn't in on it! I swear, I knew nothing about this!" I say, my heart beating fast. I try to stay calm, rational. I try to ignore their obvious disbelief. "I mean I knew him. He was my boyfriend. Dmitri. He used to come to my bar. I guess I didn't know him all that well. We've only been together a few months and—"

"You were living together," Detective Lee interrupts. "Sounds like you knew each other *fairly* well."

I try to continue. "I hadn't even seen him for three weeks. He just came back. He didn't know I had started a new job. He thought I still worked at the bar." My voice starts to rise.

"I don't know why he did this to me! I just need to talk to him, find out what happened! This is all a big mistake! I swear it! Just find Dmitri!"

"We found Dmitri Stamos," Detective Wilson says. There was something ominous in his tone.

"Wh—where is he?" I stammer, dreading the answer.

"We located him several hours after the robbery, just a few blocks from your apartment. We'd staked out the place. He was cornered. When he put up a fight, the police shot him. He's dead."

For the second time in two days, I faint.

When I come to, I find myself lying on the floor, a pillow beneath my head. The pain is raging so fiercely, I can barely focus. Again, conversations swirl around me.

"We'll book her, for second degree murder and grand larceny," I hear Detective Lee say.

"I didn't do anything," I moan softly. "I was framed."

They are not paying any attention to me.

"Effects from Dmitri Stamos. Wallet with two hundred thousand in cash. Clearly fenced the goods first. We're tracing it now." Detective Lee pauses. "And one item from Jenkins."

"Oh yeah? He kept something for himself?" Detective Wilson replies, sounding faintly curious.

"An engagement ring, still in the box." Detective Lee chuckles. "A modern Bonnie and Clyde, right here in Upper Highlands."

Stunned, I think about Dmitri's excitement the other night. *I'll have a surprise for you,* he had told me. *The start of something new...*

I bite back a bitter laugh, as the detectives haul me to my feet and read me my rights.

LEE MARVIN
Inspired by the Rhyming Slang for Starving
Travis Richardson

I'm Lee fuckin' Marvin. I've been double-crossed, shot, and I haven't eaten a damn thing in over eighteen hours. Some jobs, regardless of the payout, just aren't worth it. Not that money matters anymore. I'm getting revenge on the people who betrayed me, and then I'm going to devour a huge freakin' steak.

The night before the job, I went to the fights with my crew: Bonny, Cale, and Salvador. Everybody except my right-hand man, Knox, who stayed home to go over the job for the nineteenth time. Sipping Scotch and sucking on cigars, I made around six grand between wins and losses. Then I took my woman out for dinner and dancing. I've learned it's best not to leave an ultra-hot woman alone on Friday night or she'll find other distractions. It was close to two when we made it back to my condo and past four in the morning when Jennifer and I finished our final round of love-making.

All of this behavior before the biggest job of my life, in retrospect, borders on unprofessionality. I had carried out sixteen big-time heists without a flaw. My team and I had prepared for over a month to perfect this job. If anything, I was blowing off steam and making sure I squeezed out every ounce of juice life had to offer.

But back to my story. I woke around ten in the morning. Bleary-eyed with a hangover, but feeling great. I brewed a pot of coffee and started to whip up my infamous western egg scramble while Jennifer slept. I had all the ingredients diced, shredded, cracked, and ready to go as the cast iron pan sizzled with a bountiful pat of butter. Then a ratta-tat-tat-tat-tat pause tat-tat-tat knock came from the front door. Code from one of my crew. I grabbed a nearby Walther PK380 and slipped it in my silk robe pocket. Knox stood in the doorway, his face twisted in worry.

"You're early," I said, opening the door.

He bolted inside, shaking his head. "No, we're late. The job moved up five hours. The jet's already in the air."

I'm not known for showing strong expressions, but I think my jaw must've swung open. A little.

"Why didn't Bresson call me? Or you for that matter?"

"We did. Bresson said he called you a dozen times before calling me."

I bolted to the bedroom. Jennifer lay on her stomach, bare ass naked. I grabbed my iPhone, and dammit, the fucker was turned off. How the hell did that happen? The only time I turn it off is when I don't want a record of my whereabouts, and being in my home is the alibi that I always want to have.

I turned on the phone and walked back to the kitchen, closing the door so that Knox won't catch an eyeful of forbidden candy.

"When does the plane land?"

Knox lifted his Rolex. "In an hour and a half."

"Shit." I glanced over at the sizzling pan and the unrealized breakfast. My hangover cure wouldn't happen this morning. "Give me three minutes."

It was 10:07 a.m. I walked into the bedroom, dropped the robe, pulled up black cargo pants, squeezed into a black turtleneck, laced up my combat boots, and grabbed my pre-packed equipment bag. Looking over my shoulder, I gave Jennifer's body a brief once over and then shook out all carnal desires out of my head. All about the job now. And it was 10:10 a.m.

The crew met at a warehouse off of Jefferson Boulevard in Playa Vista. Except for Knox, we looked like shit. Cale's a weapons man, great with a gun and steady under fire. Bonny served time in Pelican Bay for a series of smash and grabs at high-end jewelry stores, but got out early on a technicality. He's athletic and quick. And Salvador's the best wheelman this side of NASCAR. I've worked with these men before and trusted them with my life. The feeling's mutual, I believe.

Putting on leather gloves, I went over the plan one more time. Then we loaded into three vehicles, each with stolen license plates. Salvador took the Town Car with a modified super engine and racing suspension. Cale and Bonny commandeered a cargo van with a reinforced steel rear bumper. I slid into a 1975 Cadillac De Ville with a five-point race harness seat belt and padded steering wheel. This unadulterated Detroit steel beast weighed over five thousand pounds. Knox strapped up in the passenger seat. We made it to the Santa Monica airport with little time to spare.

Our eyes on the ground, a young kid wanting to get into the game texted our burner phones that the private jet landed. Separated from each other by a block apiece on Ocean Park Boulevard, we knew the delivery would head north to a mansion off Mulholland Drive. We just didn't know the route the driver would take.

While we waited, my belly grumbled something fierce.

"Hungry?" Knox said with a mischievous smile.

My glare shut him up. He returned to staring out the window and shaking his nervous knee. The damn guy worried too much.

"Got a visual. They're leaving the gate now," Salvador announced over his walkie-talkie.

We started up our engines and left the curb. Salvador passed a black Chevy Surburban before it pulled onto the street. Bonny and Cale followed three to four car lengths behind. I trailed all of them almost by a block, ready to catch up to the SUV if it took on a random route. Salvador drove to the 10 freeway, anticipating our tail would use the freeways instead of surface streets. If they didn't, Salvador would double back and until he took the lead again. Fortunately, our first instinct was right, and the Suburban entered the 10 on-ramp.

Half a mile going east, Bonny and Cale's van motored past the SUV that cautiously stayed in the right lane, traveling at exactly the speed limit. Traffic was heavy westbound to the ocean, but lighter traveling toward downtown. By the time we came up to the 405 northbound on-ramp, everybody was in place. Salvador first, Bonny and Cale's van second, the mark third, and Knox and I hanging back. On the downward slope of the curving onramp where two lanes narrow to one, Bonny radioed, "Showtime."

He slammed the brakes hard. With mouth guard in place, I stomped the gas pedal to the floorboard and smashed into the rear of the Suburban. Glass exploded and metal compressed as the SUV collided into the van. Seconds later our feet hit the pavement, ski masks on. Cale opened the dazed driver's door, unlocked the rest, and threw a concussive grenade into the back.

"Fire in the hole!" he shouted.

We turned and crouched. Any glass left inside the SUV blew out as the ground beneath our feet shook. I yanked open the rear door. Two bulky bodyguards and a little man sat in the rear seat in states of semi-consciousness. I reached in and grabbed the leather attaché case off the little man's lap. His arm followed, attached via a stainless-steel handcuff to his wrist. I dragged him out of the van and onto the concrete. He blubbered nonsensical words.

"Cutters," I shouted like a surgeon with my right hand up behind me.

Knox unzipped a duffle bag and handed me a pair of bolt cutters. Two quick snips to the handle, and I'm on my feet running with the attaché case to the waiting Lincoln.

I slid into the passenger seat, while the other three loaded into the back. I dropped the attaché into a lead lined box by my feet. If a tracking device happened to be stitched inside the fine premium leather, I didn't want the signal to go out. Salvador glanced at me, eyebrows raised asking *we good?*

I nodded. "Punch it."

Salvador burned rubber as we barreled onto the 405. I noted the time on my Omega. A shade over two minutes. Could've been better, but definitely could've been a whole lot worse. We exited Santa Monica Blvd and switched to a Mercedes several blocks later. We navigated surface streets back to Playa Vista. Watching the side view mirror, nobody seemed to follow us.

Thirty minutes later we're back at the warehouse. We haven't said a word to each other. It's bad luck to celebrate until we get paid.

Inside the warehouse, I slid back the lead box and waved an electronic scanner over the attaché. It beeped. Knox handed me a knife. Gutting the bottom of the bag, a slim plastic rectangle with a wire antenna fell out. Bonny's ready with a hammer and smashed it to smithereens. A signal shouldn't have gone out in those few seconds.

Reaching inside the attaché, I pulled out a heavy purple velvet bag. Loosening the drawstring at the top of the bag, I poured out dozens of multi-carat jewels—sapphires, emeralds, rubies, diamonds—onto a folding table. The overhead light caused the walls to sparkle. The crew hunkered in close to take in the awe.

Salvador whistled. "Beautiful, man."

Bonny and Cale nodded. At that moment I realized Knox wasn't standing with us. Fear seized my heart as I whipped around. He stood twenty feet away holding a TEC-9 with an extended clip. Determination radiated from his eyes.

"Get down," I shouted, dropping to the floor.

Knox squeezed the trigger. Cale and Salvador flew backwards with blood spurting from their chests. I flipped the table over, scattering priceless stones across the concrete floor.

"The fuck, man," Knox shouted, blasting holes into my particleboard shelter.

I blindly returned fire. So did Bonny. But he was exposed, and Knox nailed him. I ran to the exit, firing my last few rounds. Throwing open the door, Jennifer stood by my Jaguar, looking gorgeous as ever. But her eyes were hard as she brought up a small caliber handgun. Ducking, I ran as two bullets flew over my head. A third bullet slammed into my back. I kept my feet moving as Knox kicked open the door and rained bullets everywhere. Scaling a chain-link fence, two more bullets hit. Gritting my teeth, I pulled myself over and rolled down an embankment into Ballona Creek.

Splashing into the raging water, I felt grateful for the previous two days of rain that turned the usually placid creek into a river. Knox and Jennifer watched from above. My former right-hand man pointed his weapon at me one more time. I gulped air and plunged under water.

Minutes later I was swimming in the ocean, trying to get out of a current. My back, thigh and shoulder burned like hell. With all the holes in me, I needed to get back to shore or I'd become shark bait. Setting my sights on a jetty, I hoped I wouldn't bleed out before I got there. I swam to boulders, exhausted and spent. Taking off my soaked clothes, I checked myself. A bullet lodged in a back rib. Probably cracked the bone too. Best to leave it alone. My right quadriceps had a nasty, bleeding crease, but nothing serious. My left shoulder, however, had the worst damage. Lifting my arm created mind-searing pain. That would be a problem. Ripping up parts of my turtleneck, I patched myself up as best I could. I considered staying on the jetty and resting for a while, but couldn't. My partner in crime for the past five years and a girlfriend of six months teamed up against me. Burning with rage, I had to get revenge.

A dark marine layer drifted in from the ocean, matching

my mood. The temperature dropped a dozen degrees, and I started shivering hard. I dove into the water and swam a sidestroke to the shore. Wearing nothing but the tied-on bandages and jockey shorts, I crawled up to the sand on the beach.

Most people ignored me as they were packing up, the cold gloom at my back chasing them home. I hoped the lifeguards at the distant station wouldn't notice me or would write me off as a crackpot homeless man and leave me the hell alone. Trudging through the sand with a painful limp, I came upon a gorgeous brunette wearing a short sweater and reading a Richard Stark novel. My kind of woman.

I stopped and scanned the horizon for Knox or Jennifer. Neither were in sight. The reader looked up and cocked her head sideways.

"Looks like you've had a hard day."

"You better believe it."

We stared at each other.

"You need a ride?"

I nodded. Without a word she closed her book, folded her blanket, and started walking. I followed feeling that any other day we might've ended up in a bedroom, getting to know each other very well. Unfortunately, revenge consumed my mind.

Her ride was a VW Beetle and not a modern one. After a backfire that nearly caused me to jump out of my seat, she navigated down the road, driving towards my condo in Manhattan Beach. I considered going to the safe house in Inglewood, but if I were Knox, that's exactly where I would go and wait in ambush for my bedraggled double-crossee to enter the threshold…that is, if I thought my victim were still alive. Of course they could also wait for me at my apartment.

"Don't you think you should go to the hospital first?"

I checked all my three wounds. Blood seeped from them and onto the towel she'd given me. While doctors would be best, alcohol and gauze should handle my immediate needs.

"I'm good. And I'm sorry about your car. I'll pay you back

for the cleaning."

She shot an eyebrow-crunching quizzical look at me.

"You talk like you're a man with a future."

"You don't think I'll make it past tomorrow to thank you properly?"

She shrugged. "Maybe. But I don't think you're a man driven by good choices."

I looked her over for the first time, reading mischief in her half-smile. "I take it you like bad boys?"

"Danger breaks up monotony, doesn't it?"

"Keeps things interesting."

She nodded with a knowing smile and turned on the radio to a jazz station playing fast tempo bebop. Who was this lady?

We drove in silence on Vista Del Mar with the Pacific on our right and screaming jets from LAX launching over our heads from the left. A few food trucks parked by Dockweiler Beach caught my eye. I fought the urge to ask this woman pull over and buy me a Korean taco. She's already put herself out enough for me.

"If I were to ask you your real name, would you give it me?" she asked.

"No. But call me John. I'll answer to that. What's your name?"

"You can call me Jenny."

I shook my head. "Nope. Try another."

She glanced over. "Hit a nerve, didn't I?"

I didn't answer.

"Fine. Do you have a history with a Nikki? That's with two Ks and an I."

I shook my head with my own half-smile, holding back a wiseass comment on the spelling. I realized my mind was drifting away from the urgent matter at hand. It was after 1 p.m., and the scheduled rendezvous with Bresson was supposed to be at 7 p.m. at a bar in Culver City. I could ambush Knox at the bar, but that would rightfully spook Bresson who would be carrying a briefcase full of money.

No, better to find out where the hell those two backstabbers were hiding and take care of business without his involvement.

Nikki asked a few more questions, but I didn't answer, focusing on what could happen in the next few hours. She understood and turned up the volume, Charlie Parker blaring a solo on his saxophone.

She dropped me off two blocks from my condo. I peered in through the passenger window.

"How can I find you to repay this kindness?"

She pulled out a pen and scrap of paper from her purse, scribbled her phone number, folded it, and handed it to me.

"If you really want to repay me, I hope it comes with a full dinner."

"You like steak?"

"Prime rib, rare."

I nodded and walked away. Listening to the Bug putter away, I changed directions and walked to my unit. Located on the third floor, it has an unobstructed view of the ocean. A neighbor did a double take as I walked through the lobby. Punching the elevator call button, I saw myself in the mirror. I looked like a gray-haired Tarzan who swam in the ocean during Navy target practice.

Stepping off the elevator, I walked to my door and stopped, hearing voices inside. Knox and Jennifer. I couldn't believe the ultra-cautious Knox would have the balls to come back to my pad after he tried to kill me. In my mind, after he shot up the creek, hoping to tag me with more lead, he would have made sure the rest of the crew was dead, collected the jewels, and hid out someplace random or set an ambush in Inglewood.

I turned the knob, surprised to find it unlocked. Easing the door open, I saw Knox with his back towards me, talking to the bedroom. Buttoning up his shirt. Hair askew. Post-coital. I understood Knox's missteps now. His mind had been muddled by Jennifer's seduction. I understood. She duped me too.

My eyes scanned the living room for any weapon. Seeing none, I crept toward the kitchen for a carving knife while listening to their conversation.

"You sure you can't move the time up with your fence?" Jennifer asked. "Maybe just ask?"

"Impossible. And stop asking. We don't need to spook Bresson any more than necessary."

"Oh, honey, I'm sorry. I just want us to get the money and fly down to Panama as fast as possible. I can't help it."

Knox shook his head, running his hands through his hair. Jennifer walked up to him wearing my silk robe. She planted a heavy kiss on him. I ducked behind the island in the kitchen. The butcher block stood against the far wall. Ten feet away. If I were healthier, I would've bum rushed them.

"Did you hear something?" Knox asked.

"No. What? You're so paranoid, Knox. Should we go for another round? I thought the first two times would've calmed your nerves."

"We shouldn't be here. When the police discover his body, they'll come here."

"Why? He has no ID. He had plastic surgery on his face. His fingerprints were altered. It'll take weeks before he's identified…and that's if they find the body which is probably a shark's lunch right now."

Knox pulled away, walking into the kitchen. I crawled around to the opposite end of the island. Dammit. So close.

Jennifer followed him. I watched their reflections from the glass on the microwave oven.

"Look, I know you're upset at what you did to him and your crew. But it's for the best. We'll never have to work another day in our lives."

"What if he isn't dead, Jennifer?"

"Impossible. I shot him. You shot him. There was all that blood…"

Considering the next weapon of choice, it would either be a bottle of wine on the counter above my head or the cast iron pan next to the uneaten ingredients for the scramble that never happened. And thinking about the breakfast caused my stomach to growl like a grizzly ripping up a campsite.

"What's that?" Knox said.

Jumping to my feet, I grabbed the cast iron pan and swung it at Knox's head. He got his left arm up in time for me to smash it. Bone crunched along with a deep iron thud. My protégé fell to the floor, howling in pain. I raised the pan over my head with my good arm. Ready to scramble Knox's brains. From my periphery, I saw Jennifer bring a pistol out of my robe pocket. I dove as a bullet slammed into the cabinet. Holding the pan out like a shield, I ran across the living room to the balcony. Two bullets dinged off the cast iron. I leaped over the side.

Falling three floors, I landed on the manicured hedges. Jennifer peered over the balcony. Her face twisted in rage. I winked and blew her a kiss. She took angry, wild shots as I limped away.

On my way to the ocean, I grabbed a wetsuit that a surfer had left out to dry on his fence. My shoulder howled in pain, but the suit fit fine and altered how people appraised me. An older surfer dude instead of a bleeding nutjob in his skivvies. A hat would help one step further, but you work with what you've got.

Hearing sirens wail in the distance I walked along the beach with my toes biting in the rough sand. Although the weather had turned cold and gloomy, it didn't stop the surfers from catching waves. I spotted towels and a bag here and there from where surfers left them behind. A few would have a car key buried nearby, but most probably carried their keys in their wetsuits. I could only be wrong a couple of times before I'd have to fight off a tribe of pissed off surfers, and I needed to preserve my energy for two other people.

I walked over to the Manhattan Beach Pier parking lot and scoped out cars and trucks that seemed like a surfer would own, yet modern enough to require a bulky electronic key that would feel uncomfortable to wear on the waves. I settled on a Toyota Tacoma with several surfing bumper stickers. Quickly finding the magnetic key box by the front bumper, I hit the road.

The truck had everything I wanted. A wallet with cash and credit cards, dry clothes, and yes, a first aid kit. After I patched up and put on jeans and a California Republic T-shirt, I headed over to a pawnshop in Culver City.

When I walked inside, the owner, Jackie Krueger, did a double take.

"Holy shit, I never thought I'd ever see you wearing a T-shirt and flip-flops. What happened?"

"Business deal gone bad. I want to see if I can get some credit."

She crossed her arms, and gave me a disapproving look. I'd known Jackie for years. Technically she sells jewelry and loans money, but most of her revenue comes from dealing firearms under the table. She's one tough woman you'd never want to double-cross. And she's unshakable about her rules.

"You know I can't do that. Cash or nothing. That even includes you."

I nodded. The surfer only had sixty dollars in his wallet. I sighed. Not enough for a gun.

"Look now," Jackie said, her eyes growing softer. "If you want to pawn that Omega on your wrist, I'm sure we could work something out."

I'd owned that SeaMaster for decades. The only item I never gave up throughout my various identity reincarnations. But considering the facts that I should be dead and I needed to get not only revenge but enough money to start over again, she was offering me a bargain I couldn't refuse.

Taking off the watch, she looked at it and then me.

"Don't worry. I won't sell it…at least for a few months."

She went into the back and came back with a shoebox. Inside was a Glock 17 with an extra clip and ammunition.

"Can you throw in a burner too?"

She grabbed a disposable phone from the wall. I nodded my thanks and walked out the door.

Armed, I drove to the safe house in Inglewood. I drove around the block three times, trying to find anything unusual. Nothing. Walking in through the back, I found the money, the IDs, and the guns were all gone. Even the canned food and energy bars were gone. Knox had cleaned me out. Everything except for a suit I found hanging up in a spare bedroom closet, still wrapped in plastic. Mine. Tailored to my exact measurements. Putting it on with a crisp white shirt and black tie, I felt like my old self. Stood tall. Shoulders back. Injuries be dammed.

I had no idea where my betrayers went, so I drove to the rendezvous place on La Cienaga Blvd, two hours before the appointed time. A hipster bar called the Mandrake. We changed locations every time. Only Knox and I knew the location that Bresson chose a couple of days before.

I sat in the back at a booth away from the bar. They don't serve food here, of course. But they have Scotch. I sipped a smoky Ardbeg Uigeadail. Pistol on my lap. Waiting, while hipsters with tattoos and Chuck Taylors shouted over the blaring music.

And that's where I'm at now. Two Scotches down, pain easing, while thinking about the revenge and the victory steak dinner with Nikki. Bresson should be here any minute.

I hear two muted cracking noises from somewhere. The bar door swings open and a girl with oversized red plastic glasses rushes inside.

"Oh my god, somebody call an ambulance. Two men have just been shot."

I'm on my feet rushing to the door. Outside in the cool

moist air, both Knox and Bresson lie on the sidewalk, twisting in agony under a streetlamp. Puddles of blood pool underneath them. A black Lexus squeals away from the curb, flying through a red light. Jennifer's behind the wheel.

I squat next to Bresson.

"What happened?"

He looks up at me, squinting in pain. "Knox walked up to me as I was entering the bar...called my name...I looked at him. A woman shot him from behind. Then she shot me... took the money and his jewels."

My brain tries to comprehend this. She has not only the money but the jewels too.

"Who else could fence the jewels?"

He shakes his head feebly, life draining away by the seconds. "Nobody...they were one of a kind...Russian...Romanov crown jewels...black market only."

Things start to piece together now.

"Who is the seller?'

"Pah..." he grunts. His eyes glaze over. Curtains for the fence.

Jennifer, or whatever her real name is, has been a plant. Not working independently. I start to run to the truck, but Knox reaches out his bloody hand. He grabs my pant leg. Looking up at me, his face unnaturally pale and eyes glistening.

"I'm sorry. So sorry—"

I kick my leg free and glare all the contempt I can muster. He shutters into a death rattle cough. I'm in the truck, heading to the 10 freeway. I'm hoping I'm not too late.

Fifteen minutes later I'm at the Santa Monica Airport again. A black Lexus double-parked by the entrance. I run up the stairs to the second-floor outdoor viewing area. A pilot inspects a Citation jet as if readying the plane for takeoff. It's a violation to land or take off in a jet plane at this airport in the evening. But wealthy people pay fines as a privilege to break the law for convenience. I lower myself down the railing.

Those wounds burn. Using pain to boost my stride. I walk over to the jet. Glock's in my hand. The pilot sees me at the last moment.

"Hey, buddy."

I bash him over the head with the pistol butt and step inside the jet. Jennifer sits in a chair with her back to me. In three quick steps I'm behind her. Before I can say anything, she slumps over. Dead. Strangled from behind.

"Bravo," a thick accented voice says behind me.

I turn my head to see a pale, lanky man emerging from the cockpit. Pytr Popov. A slime ball in the Russian underworld. He points a pistol at me.

"You used her like she used me," I say.

"But I killed her when she did not kill you. Drop the gun."

My pistol falls with a thud. In an instant I understand the Russian's entire plan.

"You sold those jewels to a black-market collector this morning, here in the airport after your plane landed."

"Yes."

"Then we stole them from the new owner, and you had Jennifer steal them back along with our payoff money."

Popov beams with pride. "Why not take two things instead of one. It's what makes me successful."

"You really think you can sell those jewels again?"

"Sure I can. I have to wait awhile, true. But I come up with a plausible story of how they came back to me. I might even sell them to the same buyer. Besides nobody breathing knows my scheme except for you and me. And that's one person too many."

"I suppose you counted all the jewels," I say casually, not showing an ounce of fear.

"What do you mean?" His head cocks in curiosity.

"There was a scuffle when Knox double-crossed me. The stones hit the floor and I grabbed a few."

Popov scrunches his face. "I'll take them off your corpse."

"They're not on me."

"You lie."

"How can you be certain?"

Popov switches the pistol to his left hand, reaches under the bar, and pulls out the attaché from a drawer. Without looking, he takes out the velvet bag. I see a briefcase—probably Bresson's payment—in the drawer.

"There should be forty-four jewels," he says. "Any less and maybe you might live. Back up two steps."

I take two half steps. He dumps the jewels on the pullout table next to Jennifer. The stones dazzle in the overhead light. Popov's mesmerized eyes widen for the second I need. With one long step, I kick the table. Priceless jewels fly in the air. Grabbing Popov's gun hand, I head butt him in the nose. He drops the pistol. I pick it up and blast five shots into him. One for each of my crew and one more for Bresson.

I scoop up a dozen jewels and grab the briefcase. Seconds later, I'm sprinting from the tarmac. I drive to Venice Boulevard, wipe down the Tacoma, and boost an old Volvo. I pull out the number I've been keeping in my skivves.

"Hello," Nikki answers.

"It's me."

"The guy named John?"

"Right now you can call me Starvin' Marvin."

"Like fuckin' Lee Marvin."

"Exactly." Holy shit. This woman knows that cockney reference. She's a keeper. "I hope you're ready to eat a big steak. Wear something nice. I'm taking you to Lowry's Prime Rib."

"I can't wait."

Today might not be so bad after all.

TROUBLE AND STRIFE
Inspired by the Rhyming Slang for Wife
Colin Campbell

"Back in Yorkshire we just call it a string vest."

"You're not in Yorkshire, you're in L.A."

Jim Grant snorted a laugh. "Yeah. Where nothing is what it seems."

The man he was talking to in a bar just off Hollywood Boulevard swiveled on his barstool and gave him a sideways glance. "Meaning?"

Grant kept his tone light. "Well, take you for instance. In America a sleeveless vest is a wife beater." His eyes hardened. "But you don't look anything like a string vest."

Jim Grant was in Los Angeles looking up his old friend Chuck Tanburro. The ex-cop turned technical advisor had been working constantly since retiring from the LAPD, putting actors through their paces and ensuring that police procedures were adhered to in TV shows and movies. Of course, this being Hollywood, if the story needed to bend the rules then police procedures went right out the window. A bit like being a cop, only without getting shot at.

Grant was down from Boston, where the Yorkshireman

had settled in with the Boston Police Department after the incident at Jamaica Plain, and was catching up with Tanburro after the trouble at Montecito Heights. Some people reckoned Grant brought a shitload of bad luck wherever he went while the press reveled in calling him The Resurrection Man, a name Grant detested.

"When are they going to get tired of calling me that?"

Tanburro leaned on an arc lamp at the edge of the movie set on Wilshire Boulevard just behind MacArthur Park. "When you stop getting into shit that keeps making the news."

"It's not the shit, it's the fact they're always filming it."

"So, keep a low profile."

Grant gave Tanburro a withering look. "You used to be a cop. Since when did catching villains keep a low profile?"

"Villains?"

"Thieves. Bad guys. Shitbags. Whatever you call them in L.A."

Tanburro wrinkled his nose. "You English are so quaint."

The clear blue sky and baking sun was anything but English.

"Our sayings or our accent?"

"Both."

Grant waved towards the makeup trailer parked next to the duck pond. "I'm not the one with a main actor basing his character on Cockney rhyming slang."

Tanburro followed Grant's gaze. "You heard about that huh?"

"I thought Hollywood had learned its lesson after Dick Van Dyke."

Tanburro shrugged. "Circle of life. Those who don't learn from history are destined to repeat it."

Grant nodded at the Westlake Theatre sign across the park. "Is that why they always film facing that way?"

Tanburro indicated the MacArthur Park Lake. "You can film a duck pond anywhere. There's only one Westlake Theatre. Even if it is a Swap Meet now."

The makeup trailer door opened and a muscle-bound hunk came down the steps followed by a fragile looking woman with big hair. The hunk flexed his shoulders and popped his biceps just in case anyone was looking. The woman kept her face down and stood behind him.

Tanburro let out a sigh. "Here he comes."

Grant was concentrating on the woman. Anyone that beautiful must have a good reason for keeping her face turned down. When they crossed the park he saw why. No amount of Hollywood makeup could hide a swollen eye or the vicious bruise down one side of her face. Even so she stayed close to the man she was obviously afraid of, twitching at every sudden movement. Tanburro noticed what Grant was looking at.

"That's his wife."

"But she won't make a complaint, right?"

"Right. He's gone full cockney. Calls her his Trouble and Strife."

Grant watched them shoot a scene where the muscle-bound hunk confronts two black kids in hoodies on the footpath surrounding the lake. The fountain was in the background with sun shining through the spray. He noted that whenever Hollywood filmed a fountain the sun was always shining through the spray. He guessed it was the same as always facing the Westlake Theatre; what made it onto the screen was what looked good not what was real. He was standing next to the catering truck where Tanburro was drinking strong black coffee.

"How come it's always two black kids in hoodies?"

Tanburro dumped a mountain of sugar into his coffee. "Because if it was Mexicans there'd be a riot."

"I thought L.A. was the home of riots."

Tanburro nodded at the muscle-bound hunk. "It's the home of wannabe actors thinking they're gonna be stars."

Grant watched the scene reset for a second take. "He's not

going to be a star?"

Tanburro put a travel lid on his coffee. "Kurt Bochner? He's going to be a pain in the ass."

"Bochner? Sounds like a German sausage."

"He wants to be a single name star. Like Eastwood or Schwarzenegger."

"Schwarzenegger *is* a German sausage."

Uniformed cops let the traffic through on Wilshire while the crew reset the camera. They were retired LAPD who looked too old for their uniforms. Grant had been surprised to learn that retired cops were allowed to keep their uniforms and sidearms and could perform traffic duty for hire. In Yorkshire you had to hand everything in when you retired or prove it had been destroyed. He remembered one constable who had to pay for his helmet even though it was the old style that had been replaced years ago.

Grant indicated the traffic cops. "You liaise with the retirees as well as give technical advice?"

Tanburro glanced at the LAPD veterans. "I liaise with everything to do with police work. Even got a doughnut shop down the way."

Grant smiled. "Is that true? The cops and doughnuts thing?"

"Makes a good story. Same as throwing your arms out like Jesus on the cross."

"That was to show the gunman I was unarmed. Not my fault Fox News was filming it."

"Doughnuts and Resurrection Men. Tall tales we live by."

Grant watched the camera crew prepare for the next take. "Is this tall tale going to be one we live by?"

"Bochner thinks so. Reality is, not a hope in hell. It's a pilot that'll never get picked up unless he creates enough publicity and gets his name in the news."

Grant watched the actor get his makeup touched up. "Maybe he should throw his arms out like Jesus on the cross."

It was Tanburro's turn to look at the woman cowering in

Bochner's shadow. "Maybe he should stop beating his wife. That kind of publicity will stop his career in its tracks."

Lights, camera, action. Bochner confronted the black kids again and the camera followed on the dolly track. Grant had lost interest in the scene being filmed though and was looking at the man's wife. "Yeah, I might have a word about that."

In the end it wasn't Bochner that Grant had a word with. The Yorkshire cop had only watched the filming to gauge Bochner's size and movement, knowing that when it comes to confrontations it's speed over size that matters, not exactly what they say in the condom adverts. Grant had made a living avoiding confrontation but knew that the best way to avoid a fight was to be able to win it if you had to. Grant wasn't going to win a fight with Kurt Bochner.

Once he'd figured that out he turned his attention to the alternative to fighting. If there was any truth in the old adage divide and conquer, there was even more in the saying hell hath no fury like woman scorned. Even if that woman was battered and bruised and scared of her own shadow. Grant decided to work on removing that shadow.

"How are you doing? Can I get you a drink?"

Lizzie Bochner, formerly Bourdon, jumped despite Grant using his most English of accents. Friendly tone and no contractions. He was never going to have a BBC voice but the Yorkshire accent often worked wonders; a bit like the softened Scottish burr that made Sean Connery the best James Bond. Grant stood on the downslope so the woman was taller than him and gave her a lazy smile.

"It must get boring watching your husband have his eye shadow retouched."

Lizzie gave him a nervous smile in return. "He doesn't use eye shadow."

Grant sat on a park bench and gestured for her to join

him. At first she seemed reluctant then responded to the smile and the accent. The camera crew was down the slope by the lake, Bochner too busy to see what his wife was doing. Sun glinted on the water, breaking up the clear blue reflection.

"That's because he puts the shadow on your eyes."

He held up a calming hand before Lizzie could back away.

"But I've got something better than makeup remover."

The movie circus was finished at MacArthur Park by five o'clock, negotiating the rush hour traffic along Wilshire Boulevard by taking cross streets and a zigzag route back to the location base. For a TV pilot that was doomed to failure the production company didn't scrimp on expense, having a heavily guarded compound opposite the Hollywood Forever Cemetery on Santa Monica Boulevard. Not exactly the Paramount Studios backlot on the other side of the cemetery but in the same zip code. The cemetery looked more like a movie set than the studio.

Grant tagged along, keeping the convoy in sight even when the lights went against him. He'd done a bit of covert observations and long tails in Yorkshire but much more with the Boston Police Department. You didn't have to follow crooks in Yorkshire because you always knew where they were going. It was a limited pool and a smaller landscape. You could drop England into California and not even notice. Following Kurt Bochner was similar to tailing the petty crooks from Bradford, Bochner had a limited range and Grant knew where he was going anyway.

A news helicopter thudded overhead, drifting towards West Hollywood and Studio City. Grant kept his eyes on the prize and refused to glance up at the bane of his life, 24-hour news coverage. Another helicopter raced across the sky in the opposite direction. He was surprised there weren't more midair collisions, the skies above Los Angeles being almost as busy as downtown Manhattan.

The convoy skirted the cemetery then turned into Bronson Avenue just past the Omega Cinema Props parking lot. The production vehicles snaked into the compound and began to line up in the cleared area beside a port-a-cabin office. The retired LAPD cops did traffic duty again, keeping the vehicles moving while appeasing angry commuters. They didn't take much appeasing, with armed men in uniform waving their hands at them.

Grant pulled into a strip mall opposite the Dearly Departed Tours and Artifacts Museum, a sign in the window advertising Cemetery Maps Available Here. The makeup trailer and craft services truck were the last into the compound. Five minutes later a Chevy Suburban with blacked out windows came through the gates and headed towards Hollywood and Vine.

Just as expected. The most successful police operations were the ones with the best intelligence. Grant's intelligence told him where Bochner was going next. There was no need to rush. He was going to savor this.

O'Neil's Bar reminded Grant of Flanagan's in Jamaica Plain, small and dark with red brick interior walls and a full-length bar mirror. It was up the hill from Hollywood Boulevard on Vine Street between the antique cinema frontage of Avalon Hollywood and a 7-Eleven and just down from the Capitol Records building across the road. The Suburban was parked opposite with the courtesy driver lounging against the steering wheel. Grant dismissed him as not a threat and went inside.

Yes, the interior was just like Flanagan's. Maybe all bars with Irish names went for the same theme, rundown and dingy but with every shade of whisky. There were booths along the left-hand wall and tables in the front window and barstools all the way along the carved wood bar. A couple of workmen still wearing coveralls sat in the second booth from the end and three women sat at a window table, watching the world go by in between incessant chatter. The barman was polishing glasses near the cash register. Barmen always seemed to be polishing glasses if they weren't serving customers.

Kurt Bochner was sitting on the end barstool next to the restroom passage. He looked up when Grant came in but didn't recognize him. The actor looked slightly put out that nobody was fawning over him and went back to nursing his drink. Grant glanced at the restroom passage then at the two workmen. No threats there either. If any trouble started it was the barman who would step in and stop it. That was something else they did when they weren't serving customers. Grant smiled and gave him a wave to get him on his side. Barmen seldom hit a man who is smiling.

"Before I ask, is it Coca Cola or Pepsi? Because whenever I ask for Coca Cola they only stock Pepsi and vice versa."

The barman stopped polishing. "It's beer and whisky."

Grant walked up to the bar. "Sounds like a song I once heard." He strangled his singing voice. "Cigarettes and whisky and wild, wild women. They'll drive you crazy, they'll drive you insane."

The barman nodded at the door. "Cabaret's down the street."

Grant rested soft hands on the bar. Not fists. "I'm driving, so could I have a Coca Cola please?"

"We only have Pepsi."

Bochner laughed and Grant threw his hands out in surrender. The barman couldn't keep a straight face any longer. His leathery features broke into a smile.

"Just kidding. We got Coke."

Grant smiled in return. "Well, that broke the ice. I'm Jim Grant." He turned to Kurt Bochner. "And you're that guy on TV aren't you?"

***

They settled in pretty quick after that, Grant with his Coca Cola and Bochner with his fifty shades of whisky. The workmen kept talking work and the ladies just kept talking. The barman went back to polishing glasses. Grant sat on the next available barstool; the one next to the second-rate actor and two down from the passage to the restrooms and the back door.

Grant rubbed his chin. "Don't tell me. Your name's on the tip of my tongue." He stopped rubbing and snapped his fingers. "Hart Butcher."

"Bochner."

"Hart Bochner? That weasely fuck in *Die Hard*?"

"Kurt Bochner. And just call me a weasely fuck again. Go on."

Grant held his hands up again. "Sorry. Not you obviously." He took a sip of his Coke. "He'd be sixty plus by now. But I have seen you before."

Bochner looked torn between bragging and embarrassment. "Done a couple of commercials. Some bit parts in *CSI* and *NCIS*. Played a dead body once."

Grant feigned distaste. "Urgh. Dead people. No thanks."

Bochner showed he had a sense of humour. "Not many lines."

Grant laughed. "I guess not. What you working on now?"

Bochner brightened up. "Shooting a pilot for Netflix. Cop show where this PTSD soldier back from the war gets recruited by LAPD."

Grant shivered again. "PTSD? Gives you a chance to unleash your inner demons, I'll bet." He brought his fists up in a boxing pose and threw a few shadow punches. "Hit people in the face."

"This is the movies. We don't hit people in the face. We aim to miss, just set the camera angle so it looks like we connect."

"No hitting in the face then?"

"No."

"You come straight from the set? 'Cause unless you dress in ladies clothes you've still got your makeup on."

Bochner rubbed his cheek then checked his fingers. "Oh yeah. Left my high heels in the restroom."

Grant's eyes widened as if he'd just remembered something. "I read about that Netflix thing. PTSD Cockney. Comes out with all this rhyming slang."

Bochner looked pleased that someone had heard of the show. "That's right. Been watching *The Sweeney* to get my head right."

"Loaf. Not head. Loaf of bread."

"Yeah."

"The TV series not the movie I hope."

"There was a TV show?"

"Would you Adam and Eve it? You didn't know about the TV series?"

"Adam and Eve it. Believe it. Good."

Grant took another swig of his Coke. "I knew cops back in Yorkshire, detectives mainly, used to model themselves on *The Sweeney*. Either that or *The Sweeney* got it bang right. Always getting Brahms and Liszt and falling down the Apples and Pears."

"Pissed and stairs."

"Whenever they had to search a villain's house it was always, 'Let's go spin his drum.' We never call it that in Yorkshire. It's just a house search."

"Life imitating art."

"Amen to that."

A young couple came in off the street and sat at the other end of the bar. Smartly dressed. Young. Either business types or Jehovah's Witnesses. The way the young man was eyeing the woman's cleavage, Grant dismissed Jehovah's Witnesses. Work colleagues maybe, with the man wanting it to be something more. The barman went down to serve them, giving Grant and Bochner a little privacy. Grant put his glass down and leaned in.

"L.A. being the home of the weird and wonderful, I'm sure

you've got plenty of sayings yourself."

Bochner shrugged. "L.A.'s home for everyone. Most cosmopolitan city in the world. We've got sayings from everywhere."

"America in general then."

"Yeah. We've got a few."

Grant lowered his voice. "Sleeveless vests and suchlike. Back in Yorkshire we just call it a string vest."

"You're not in Yorkshire, you're in L.A."

Grant snorted a laugh. "Yeah. Where nothing is what it seems."

Bochner braced his shoulders, flexed his muscles then swiveled on his barstool and gave Grant a sideways glance. "Meaning?"

Grant kept his tone light. "Well, take you for instance. In America a sleeveless vest is a wife beater."

His eyes hardened. "But you don't look anything like a string vest."

If they settled in pretty quick after the Coke and the whisky, things got unsettled real quick after the string vest joke. The barman was still serving the couple down the other end of the bar. The workmen were still talking work and the women were still talking. The only oasis of quiet was the two barstools next to the restroom passage.

Grant leaned back in his seat but the barstool wouldn't let him get out of Bochner's fighting arc. He kept the glass of Coca Cola handy in case he needed a drink in the face distraction. The other way to keep from getting hit in the face was to smile. Grant kept the smile on his face and his tone light but the words were getting stronger.

"You being in a cop show, I'm sure you know this already, but here's the thing. With all this Me Too movement in Hollywood, the police have had to move with the times. Make it easier to report abuse and less stressful giving evidence. Back in the day, it was only kids who could give evidence by video link but now…"

Grant held his hands out, palms up. "Well, now, woman with one eye swollen shut, she doesn't have to give evidence at all. None of that facing your abuser shit that used to scare victims off. It's a whole different landscape. Just ask Harvey Weinstein."

Grant took a sheaf of papers from his inside pocket and smoothed them out on the bar. Typed pages with thick black signatures at the top and bottom. Stapled together in the top left-hand corner. Witness statements. More than one. "You see, from what I remember back in Yorkshire, domestic abuse was always one person's word against another. Same as non-consensual sex. If it happens in the privacy of your own home, there're no witnesses. But get a woman, your wife for instance, going into a room looking beautiful then coming out half an hour later with a black eye and swollen face. If you can prove there was only one other person in the room at the time, with CCTV or witnesses for instance, then you've pretty much got an open and shut case."

Bochner sat frozen to the spot, face like stone and holding his breath. His eyes tried to hide the fact that he was running calculations and coming up empty. Grant slid the statements across the bar but the actor didn't look at them. Grant stood up, keeping the barstool between him and the wife beater.

"If this was a Western, the bar scene with a card game and a piano player, this is the part where the music stops."

He swept a hand in a swirling motion to include the entire bar but mainly to get Bochner used to the movement. The workmen had stopped talking work and the women just stopped talking. The barman stopped polishing glasses. The couple down the far end of the bar was looking at the confrontation taking place next to the restroom passageway.

Grant gave the smile a sad inflection. "Quiet isn't it?"

Bochner was going red from the neck up. Grant couldn't

tell if it was anger or embarrassment so he kept his distance and scooped the statements up. He folded them and put them in his pocket. "Other movie clichés I like. The prison movie. There's always one guy with LOVE and HATE tattooed on his knuckles. For hitting people in the face with."

He stopped smiling.

"Want to know what mine would say?"

The barman had somehow come halfway towards them, his hands reaching under the bar. The couple went out the front door. The women stared open-mouthed but the workmen just stared, watching to see which way this was going to go. Not getting involved one way or the other. They looked to be leaning towards a big guy victory.

Bochner stood up, towering over Grant. "Trouble and Strife?"

The actor balled his fists and they looked like they could slam through the carved wood bar. Grant stepped out from behind the barstool, giving Bochner a clear shot if he wanted to take it. The time for smiling was over but there was still wriggle room for a non-violent outcome. Delaying tactics.

"That's seven letters and six. I've only got four knuckles per fist."

Bochner's eyes fogged over as if he were counting.

Grant kept him off balance. He brought his fists up like a boxer bringing up his guard. Bochner stepped away from his barstool into the mouth of the passageway, relaxing his knees and shaking out his hands. Ready to move. Grant gave a little nod towards the back door.

"No, these aren't Trouble and Strife. They are."

The two cops came out of the shadows and snapped the cuffs on Bochner so fast the actor didn't know what happened. He thought about struggling but realized he'd been outmaneuvered.

Grant lowered his hands and the smile returned. "*The Sweeney* you say? You'll have heard this before then. You're nicked."

***

Being arrested outside the toilets wasn't the coup de grace; that came when the uniformed cops walked Bochner out the front door. The thudding helicopter blades were deafening as they hovered over Vine Street, drifting south so the news crew could get the disgraced celebrity and the Capitol Records building in the same shot. A bit like always filming MacArthur Park facing the Westlake Theatre. You could film a wife beater anywhere.

To add insult to injury, the beaten wife was standing outside O'Neil's with a female officer, her swollen face turned towards the camera. A 24-hour news not only had the hulking actor but his diminutive wife in the same shot. It couldn't have been any worse if he'd been caught with his pants down getting Brahms and Liszt while falling down the Apples and Pears. A touch of creative license there if you like, but this was Hollywood. Grant was sure the news would come up with something equally cheesy.

The helicopter came around for the frontal angle as Grant followed the cops out of the bar. Bochner didn't struggle. He didn't give his wife a hard stare because he was too busy trying to keep his head down and save his career. Grant watched the arresting officers duck Bochner into the backseat of a marked unit then glanced across the street where two more cops were holding back a small crowd.

Grant nodded at the man standing to one side behind the police line. Tanburro nodded back. The helicopter stayed low just long enough for Grant to smile at Robin Citrin and wave at the woman who had tried to make him a reality TV star during the Montecito Heights incident. Bochner didn't notice that the helicopter wasn't 24-hour news. He didn't wonder about the cops looking like they were past retirement age either.

***

The next time Grant talked with Lizzie Bochner, formerly Bourdon, her face was clear and she looked a lot happier. It was two weeks later on a bench at Griffith Observatory with all of Los Angeles laid out below. The Hollywood sign looked in need of some paint but Grant reckoned that was L.A. all over, faded and past its prime. The sun was warm but hadn't burned off the smog that turned downtown L.A. into a Michael Bay filter shot.

Grant sat beside Lizzie and gave her an ice cream from the vendor. He tried not to let his drip on his trousers in the California heat. "He giving you any trouble?"

"You know he isn't."

"But you're still with him."

"You know that too."

"Yes. I bet it's hard to turn down the perks of Hollywood life."

Lizzie nibbled the soft bits around the edge of the cone. "He's just happy you managed to get them to shelve the news footage. I guess being The Resurrection Man has its perks as well."

"It's not what you know it's who you know."

"But shelved can become un-shelved. Is that the deal?"

Grant licked his ice cream. When he was sure he'd beaten the drip factor he turned to face her. "Your choices are your business. Stay or go. It's up to you. But just remember this."

A piece of ice cream he'd missed plopped onto his trouser leg.

"You don't need a string vest in Hollywood."

LADY FROM BRISTOL
Inspired by the Rhyming Slang for Pistol
Sam Wiebe

Just their luck: a woman collapsed before takeoff. The plane was held for two hours, first waiting for the paramedics and their narrow wheelchair, then waiting for an opening on the runway. Jamie was pissed. Barry kept his headphones on, listening to some podcast, what did it matter being his approach to things.

As a consequence, they were late landing in Glasgow and barely caught the last train to Stirling. They'd missed their meeting with the Poet. It wasn't a lock that they'd be able to schedule another.

After another hour spent by the phone in their hotel room, near the university, they were told to head to the Wallace Pub. If the Poet could make it, he would.

"Wait how long?" Jamie asked.

"Even if ah knew ah wouldnae tell," was the reply.

The pub was a half-hour walk. Rain was light but persistent. It felt different than American rain. Clingier, more insinuating, Jamie thought.

It was dark but they could make out the spire of the Wallace monument. The pub was close to its base.

"Kind of effect you think it has, growing up near a thing

like this?" Barry asked.

"Whole country's full of monuments and ruins. We had another day I'd take you to my family's castle."

"The Lord ancestral home?"

"Laird, but it's still us. I guess."

Barry had worn sneakers and they squelched as he walked. Jamie's Doc Martens were holding up better. At the door of the pub they knocked water from their shoes by kicking the door and siding.

Inside was small and well-heated. A few tables. Board games and books on a shelf. A bar, three old men sitting along its corner, talking to the bartender.

"An old person pub," Barry said with some delight.

They ordered pints of Deucher's, shepherd's pie and cottage pie, and took a table in the corner, Jamie sitting with his back to the wall. Barry pulled the table out and struggled into his seat, but found it comfortable once he was in.

"Funny thinking this is where our fortune could be made," he said.

My fortune, Jamie silently corrected. Barry worked for him. A friend from high school and a good head for numbers, but not worldly or ambitious. Smart but not street smart. Not *wise*. Not that Jamie saw himself as wise—but at twenty-six, poised to take over the Syracuse market, he must be doing something right.

It all depended on the Poet, if what they'd heard was true about him.

"Should we ask them?" Barry said, pointing over his shoulder at the old men at the bar.

"Nah. When he wants, he'll show himself."

"Just, we don't know what he looks like. Could be one of them, all we know."

"The Poet is young. Our generation or close to it. Darren McCousland *Junior*, remember?"

"Junior by itself doesn't mean young, Jamie."

"But you remember the story. How he was in school. Dropped out to take over for his father. That was, what, four years ago? So he's our age, 'less he was a mature student."

Barry gave up, turned his attention to the décor on the walls. William Wallace paraphernalia. The monument was lit up like a gold-tipped sword.

After a while the door opened. A young woman, pregnant, told one of the old men it was time. Her father, Jamie supposed. On their way out she got caught up talking to the bartender. Fifteen minutes later they took their leave.

A nice way to live, Jamie thought. Hang with your friends till your daughter comes to collect you. Football games and church socials. Your kids doing fine. *Their* kids developing. Jamie had two of his own. He'd done things to keep them safe and keep himself in their lives. If his plans with the Poet worked out, he'd never have to worry about them.

The Poet didn't have children. From what Jamie had heard, the Poet was gay. He'd been at Trinity studying literature when his father had been killed. Darren McCousland, Sr. was a feared man, who'd run a razor gang in Glasgow before taking over Northeast England. A drunken collision and a heart attack had put McCousland Sr.'s rackets up for grabs, with two of his older lieutenants vying for control.

The Poet had grown up away from the business. His father had wanted him separate from the gangster life, and his own inclinations seemed to recommend it. His aptitude bent towards poetry. He'd had his work published in several prestigious but unread journals. Jamie had thought of tracking one down, bringing it with him, but thought that was too kiss-ass.

The Poet had taken a ferry back from Dublin for his father's funeral. He'd stayed. Within three months he'd quelled the gang war and brought his father's people to heel. More than that—he'd expanded into both Irelands, into Wales, and was looking for partners overseas.

It made sense. Syracuse wouldn't be a large market for the

Poet, but it would be one more stream of income. With Brexit and everything else going on, it made sense to explore all the markets you could.

Their food arrived. They ordered another round. Jamie salted and peppered his pie before stirring part of the crust into the glop below.

"Goddamn that's good," Barry said. "So far, I gotta say I like this country better than England."

"'Cause they make a better meat pie?"

"The food's only part of it. The English, they have a weird hate-on for fat people."

"Do they," Jamie said, thinking Christ. Barry's woman had introduced him to the concept of fat activism. Should've introduced him to a fucking elliptical, Jamie thought. Or maybe a muzzle.

"You think about the English," Barry said, "the debt they owe fat people. Their best-known king. Best-known prime minister. All their best writers, like the dictionary guy. And the hatred they feel to us! Jenn and me were watching this comedy special, that guy from their version of *The Office*. Bit after bit about how evil it is to be a different size—and from a Lorax-looking motherfucker like him. But that's who those people are. Hate their own kind. Hate anything different. The Scottish are more accepting."

"Let's hope the Poet is," Jamie said. "None of that nonsense when he shows."

"It's not nonsense, Jamie, it's what's called microaggressions."

"Whatever it is, keep quiet about his people when he comes. Understand?"

Barry wound down. They finished their meal. Ordered a third and then a fourth. One of the other old men left, and the bartender began wiping things down.

"Y'know William Wallace had a belt made out of the skin of his enemy?" Barry said. "Had lots of stuff made out of skin, what I read."

"Mel Gibson left that out of the film," Jamie said.

"I don't think it was historically accurate."

"Great fight scenes, though."

"The battlefield over there, Stirling? 'Parently it was some guy's farm till the movie came out. All this—the monument—it's all on account of the film."

"I don't believe that," Jamie said. "Scots love history."

"Well, Mel didn't. That scene where he's rushing towards the English, and he's got nothing in his hands, then suddenly he's got this big-ass sword?"

"Continuity error, probably," Jamie said.

"He's holding an axe at one point, too, right? Some sort of club?"

"Well he probably ditched that, then started running, then picked up the sword when he found it."

"From the middle of a battlefield before the battle starts?"

"Maybe one of his guys planted it there. Or passed it to him." Jamie was tired, a little drunk. "Maybe Mel didn't know so he shot it all three ways and it's like use your own judgment."

"People here probably get asked this shit all the time, right?"

Barry turned in his chair and waited till the bartender was near the end closest to them. "'Scuse me, ma'am? What was William Wallace carrying at the Battle of Stirling? Like what kind of weapon?"

"Ha'n't the foggiest." The bartender was maybe fifty, pretty, hair gone to silver and steel. She pointed at the window in the rough direction of the monument. "His sword's in there. Ah hadtae guess it'd be that."

"You've seen *Braveheart*?" Barry asked. "What'd you think?"

She shrugged. "It's nae *Lethal Weapon*."

"Hey, you ladies from Bristol?" It was the lone man left at the bar. At least seventy, his chin a sagging, receding cliff face ending in a jowly neck. Bald with a dark pencil moustache that might've been dyed that color. His accent sounded English, slurred with drink.

The man stood, unsteady, and asked the question again. "You ladies from Bristol? How 'bout you, big boy?"

"Leave 'em be, Tommy," the bartender said.

"Just being friendly. Big boy doesn't mind."

"Actually," Barry said, "it's not appreciated."

"Wha? Being called Big Boy? It's a term of affection for husky fellas like yourself."

"Fat," Barry said. "You can say fat. There's no shame attached to that word."

"Whitever ye say, fat fuckin' bastard."

The old man launched his drink at Barry, half a pint slapping against his face and stomach.

Barry reached for him, Jamie on his feet now, not sure to interject or help, or if the booze would let him do either. The bartender had seized Tom's shoulder and was rushing him to the door. Apologizing on his behalf, telling Barry he could wash up in the sink. "Bog's behind ye, and last round's on me."

"And mine's on him," the man said gleefully. Then the door shut. The bartender stood there, waiting till Barry stalked off towards the washroom.

"Tommy's no usetae new faces," she said to Jamie. "He figgered ye for tourists."

"You get a lot of tourists?" Jamie asked. He handed her currency to pay the bill.

"Some," she said. "More in the summer."

"On account of the history of this place, or on account of the movie?"

The bartender smiled. "Ah havnae taken a poll," she said. "Wi' the Americans, ah expect, it's more fae the film."

"That bother you?"

"Havnae thought aboot it much, tae be honest. Did that lassie leave the kitchen light on? Silly cow."

She headed towards the Staff Only door, brushing past Barry coming out of the washroom.

"You ready?" Jamie asked. He wanted a cigarette and sleep. Then a shower and a nice breakfast with lots of eggs.

He was facing the door, then spun, sinking. Confused.

Barry fired again, his second shot driving a small hole through Jamie's nose that broke through his skull and tunneled into brain matter, coming to a stop close to where the first one rested after drilling through his temple.

There was no need for a third, Jamie hadn't seen or felt the second, but once he was face down on the floor Barry pulled the trigger of the .22 again. He could see blood matted in his friend's hair. Such a small amount, he thought.

"All good?" he called.

The bartender came back from the kitchen, pushing a steel cart. Together they got Jamie's body on it.

"Ter clock what kind of people I'm ter do business wif," the Poet had told him. "Fin' ya can 'andle a Lady from Bristol?"

"A lady from Bristol?"

"A pistol, son. A pistol."

"Yeah, I can handle a gun."

It was less about Jamie being a possible snitch—these days, who wasn't?—and more about a demonstration of character. Barry assumed he'd passed.

If not, he thought, this wasn't a bad country to go out in.

PLEASURE AND PAIN
Inspired by the Rhyming Slang for Rain
Robert Dugoni

I didn't plan to spend my European honeymoon alone, but when you're fiancée doesn't show up for the wedding, you have non-refundable airline tickets, and you've already had your two-week vacation request approved at work, well, you make lemonade out of lemons, as my mother would say. My father was never so diplomatic.

"Cowboy up and leave your panties at home," he told me in the alcove of the church when Anna's father called to say his daughter had had a change of heart—a profoundly interesting way to put it.

"No sense wasting a perfectly good trip," my father continued, meaning well. "What else are you going to do, sit at home and mope? Her loss. Your gain. See the world, have an adventure."

And so, the morning after what should have been my wedding night, I boarded a flight from Seattle to Frankfurt alone—more leg room for me—and, as Dierks Bentely recommended, *I got drunk on the plane.* Actually, I was drunk when I got on the plane. I just got more drunk. It wasn't exactly Mari Gras up in the clouds as Bentely sang—I eventually passed out, and when I did come down I had the mother of all headaches, and an attitude so sour I could have been sucking on those lemons my mother had talked about.

My plan that morning had been to pick up a rental car in Frankfurt and drive roughly four hours to Hohenschwangaue, Germany. It might sound a bit ambitious for two newly married honeymooners, but I had an ulterior motive. Hohenschwangaue was where King Ludwig II of Bavaria commissioned the Cliffside castle, Neuschwanstein, in 1868. With its towers, turrets, frescoes and throne hall, Neuschwanstein looks like it was plucked straight from your favorite fairy tale. In fact, the opposite is true. Walt Disney modeled Cinderella's castle at his iconic theme park after Neuschwanstein. A hopeless romantic, I had intended to surprise Anna with a trip to the castle from her favorite fairy tale.

Turned out the surprise was on me.

Maybe my choice of Neuschwanstein was more apropos of my situation than I cared to admit. It seems old King Ludwig never actually got to live his fairy-tale. He got his ass kicked in the 1866 Prussian war and died under mysterious circumstances weeks before the castle's completion. Rumors also circulated that he was insane. The same could be said for a twenty-four-year-old man traveling Germany alone on his honeymoon.

I lifted the bottle of German beer I'd bought at a gas station along the drive. "Here's to fairytales that don't come true, Ludwig," I said and took a pull, draining the bottle. "I'm on my Goddamn honeymoon," I shouted in the empty Volvo. "I'm making lemonade out of lemons. I'm pulling up my panties and Cowboying up…ping. So giddy-Goddamned up!"

As if the pounding in my head and the rip in my heart weren't enough, the weather had also turned sour, or Seattle-like. As I followed my GPS's instructions along Highway A7 I noted clouds as dark and foreboding as any Seattle could conjure, rolling in over the hills and threatening to suffocate Germany's infamous Black Forest, which is believed to be the inspiration for many of the Grimm Brothers' tales. I'd checked the weather app on my phone at my last bathroom break and, sure enough, it seemed I had indeed brought the Seattle weather with me. "Rain with a chance of more rain," I said aloud. Or as my British grandfather from London's East End would have said in his thick cockney accent, "Pleasure and pain."

The pain and the rain I could relate to. It was the pleasure I'd always had trouble with, and never more so than on this evening drive. I wondered if "drunk as a skunk" was another of the cockney rhyming slang and, if not, I thought it should be synonymous with "foul" which was definitely my mood.

The sun set at just after seven on this early April evening and I soon found, as I drove the winding road, that the rain in Germany was nothing like the rain in Seattle and they didn't call it the Black Forest for nothing. Unlike Seattle, where drizzle all day qualified as rain, in Germany the rain left no doubt. It fell from the sky in torrents. I had the windshield wipers swiping at their highest setting and I was still having trouble seeing out the windshield.

As I came around a bend in the road lightning sheeted, illuminated the gray clouds, a brilliant flash of color that, for the briefest of moments, allowed me to see Neushwanstein. Ludwig had built his castle on the top of a mountain still flecked with lingering winter snow. It was glorious.

"I'll be damned," was all I could muster before the thunder detonated—a loud throng that sounded directly over me and left my ears ringing a German symphony that would have impressed Beethoven or Brahms—or some other German composer.

"Son of a bitch," I said. "It's all fun and games until old Richie's car gets lit up like a Christmas tree."

As lightning crackled and emerged from the cloud layer in barren spindly tree branches, and the thunder exploded without reprieve, I decided the castle could wait another day, or honeymoon perhaps, and took the first exit I came to. My GPS loudly protested and insisted that I reroute, spewing out directions until I turned it off.

Peering out the windshield, I searched for shelter from the rain, money being no object. I'd saved five thousand dollars for my honeymoon and I was determined to spend every euro on wine, women and debauchery, or at least a comfortable place to sleep.

The exit, however, had deposited me on a two-lane road that plunged me deeper into the Black Forest. After fifteen minutes, without a town or even a street lamp in sight, I pondered turning around and getting back on my original course. Just as I had that thought, however, I emerged from the wall of trees and noted fence posts strung with barbed wire, an indication of civilization. A town couldn't be far, could it? Beyond the fencing, tall green grass swayed and swirled in the storm's gusting wind. I looked for animals, or at least the shadow of animals—cows or sheep or, I don't know, llamas perhaps, but if any had been in the field they'd had the good sense to get out of the deluge, something I now wished I had done hours earlier. Cinderella's castle—by myself, what the hell had I been thinking?

I continued navigating the winding road, left then right, a horseshoe turn, back the other way. I searched for a street sign, lamp post, or other indication of human habitation. Lightning struck and I shifted my eyes to the bruised colored sky for just a brief instance, but in that instance I heard and felt a sickening thump. By the time my gaze had shifted back to the road a blurred shadow whizzed past my driver's side window.

"Shit!" I hit the brakes, the car skidding to a stop. Rain beat down on the roof of the car and the wiper blades hummed a staccato beat.

I had no idea what I had hit, but was certain I had hit something. The headlights illuminated the rain, big, heavy droplets that slanted right to left with each gust. I took a deep breath, exhaled, and looked in the driver's side and my rearview mirror. The darkness prevented me from seeing anything beyond the back of the car. I wanted to drive on, but the boy in me, the one who'd grown up with animals, wouldn't allow me to do so. What if I'd hit a dog and it was lying along the side of the road, hurt?

I drove the rental forward and pulled partially into a culvert, left the engine running and the headlights on, and grabbed my dark blue Gore-Tex jacket from the passenger seat. I quickly slipped it on, pulling the hood over my head. Then I flicked the screen of my phone with my finger, hit the flashlight icon, and pushed out of the car.

The damage to the front fender and grill was more than I had anticipated. I'd hit something all right, and based on the damage it hadn't been Fido. More likely I'd hit a deer. I didn't know the extent of the damage to the engine, but at least there was no steam spewing out from under the hood, which made reaching the next town, if one actually existed, still a likely possibility.

Something caught my attention and I reached to dislodge a clump wedged in the grill. It looked like dead grass. I lowered it to the car's headlights to better view it. The strands of yellow-brown hair were of differing lengths, more a mat of hair, and not what I would have expected had I hit a deer, though I was far from an expert on the subject. I didn't even like to kill spiders. I wasn't squeamish. It just seemed to me that everything had a right to live. I usually trapped them and released them outside. Call me a wuss. I don't care.

I shone the light of my phone on the darkened road behind me, but it did little to dent the foreboding blanket of ink-black night. I could see where the Black Forest got its name. The Germans were so damned practical. I stepped to the side of the road and walked along the edge, back the direction I had driven. Water dripped from the small visor of my hood and I could feel the rain finding gaps in my outer shell. I looked for prints in the dirt—okay, I was actually looking for a deer carcass, but barring that, I looked for hoof prints. Twenty yards behind where I had stopped my car, I reached the tall grass with the fence posts and barbed wire. I looked for signs of a wounded animal, blood or where something had trampled the grass. I saw no such evidence. About to turn away, I noticed something on the barbed wire. I stepped across the small culvert and climbed the slope to the wire. There I removed another clump of hair.

As I examined the tuft, I heard a sound above the splatter of falling rain. I froze, listening intently. I heard the nose again, but what the hell was it? The third time I deciphered a low, guttural growl. Had I hit a dog? Was it lying in the thick grass? Shit, that's all I needed, to have killed some family pet. I stepped to the edge of the field of grass, shining my light, squinting against the rain and the darkness and heard another growl, this one louder, or perhaps closer?

I took a step back from the fence.

The growling intensified. I looked to the grass, from where the sound seemed to be emanating. Was it the growl of a wounded animal, or a predator? Did they have predators in the Black Forest? Bears? Cougars? Mountain lions?

I didn't know, and I wasn't looking to become some evidence of proof. I'd tell the rental company I'd hit a deer and be done with it.

About to turn and retreat down the slope to the road, movement in the grass caught my attention. The blades continued to sway in the gusts of wind, but I saw what looked to be a path in the grass, except the blades were not falling away from me. They were falling toward me. And as that realization struck, so did another. The path was not being made by something attempting to flee, but by something seeking to attack, and, whatever it was, it was closing ground fast.

Another growl, this time louder, more distinct.

Shit.

I turned, my brain having already told my feet to run, slipped and slid down the hill on my ass. My shoes plunged into the water in the culvert. I got up. Heard the growl and glanced over my shoulder, then turned for the road. Lights blinded me. I heard the squeal of brakes and the skid of tires struggling to grip wet pavement. A moment later I felt like a croquet ball smacked with an enormous mallet, the blow knocking me off my feet and propelling me backward.

I struck pavement and rolled.

My body felt like a battered piñata. The pain was bad enough that I didn't immediately try to sit up. I was clearly disoriented and confused. As my senses slowly came back online, I realized I wasn't staring up at a cloud-darkened sky spitting rain at me. I was staring up at a box-beam ceiling. In my peripheral vision I noted blurred faces, several of them, hovering above and around me. I could differentiate men from women, but that only added to the confusion. I had no idea where I was or how I had got there.

My confusion quickly became anxiety and I started to sit up, but felt the gentle pressure of a hand on my chest. My head felt like a cannon ball weighing me down.

"Easy," a woman said. "You do not wish to get up quickly."

Her voice was heavily accented. German I deduced, unless the blow of whatever had hit me—a car I presumed—had knocked me back to Switzerland, or perhaps to France. Geography had never been my strong subject in school.

"Where am I?" I barely recognized my raspy, weakened voice.

The woman said something in German. Then to me she said, "You are in Bierengarten. How is it that you feel?"

I sat up, this time getting as far as my elbows. Several pairs of hands assisted me to a sitting position that allowed me to consider my surroundings. I'd been lying on a wooden table, with someone's jacket balled into a makeshift pillow beneath my head. Around the room candle flames flickered in their holders along the wall, illuminating about two dozen men and women seated or standing near sturdy but nicked and scarred wooden tables and benches. Carefully, I swung my legs over the table's edge and, with help, eased down onto a wooden bench. Someone handed the woman a glass and she handed it to me. I sipped cool water then set the glass on the table. The men and women stared at me as if awaiting a papal blessing.

"What happened?" I asked. "How did I get here?"

An elderly man stepped to the edge of the table. Balding, he had a ring of white hair and a concerned expression, though concern for me or for himself I couldn't tell. He wore a raincoat that extended past his knees to the tips of rubber boots, and he kneaded a tweed cap in his hands. "You were standing in the middle of the road," he said. "I couldn't see you. The lights of your car blinded me when I came around the bend. By the time I saw you…"

"Ernst hit you with his truck." The woman completed Ernst's sentence for him. "Luckily he saw you in enough time to hit his brakes, but the pavement was slick from the rain."

"You hit your head," Ernst said.

I reached up and felt a knot on the back of my head, painful to the touch, which explained the headache. "What about the animal?" I asked.

The woman glanced at the others, a quick twitch. Ernst shook his head and shrugged. "I don't know."

"I hit an animal…a deer I think. That's why I was out of my car. I got out to see what I'd hit. That's why my car was parked on the side of the road."

"There was nothing," Ernst said.

"I hit an animal with my car," I repeated. "I got out to see if I could find it." The night came back to me in bits and pieces. "I heard it. I heard a growl."

"I found nothing," Ernst said. "I carried you here in my truck. Emma said to put you on the table."

"Do you need for a hospital?" the woman, whom I presumed to be Emma, asked.

I contemplated Emma's question before deciding that, though sore, nothing seemed to be broken. After a minute to further get my bearings I said, "No. I'm all right."

"Get him a beer," a portly man in a white T-shirt covered by a long apron said. The proprietor of this establishment, I presumed.

"Could it have been a bear, or perhaps a mountain lion?" I asked those gathered around me, but my question went unanswered.

"Are you hungry?" Emma asked.

"No. No I don't think so." I inhaled and exhaled several times. "I think I'd better just get going."

"You won't be going anywhere tonight," the man in the apron said. "Power is out and so too is the road."

"What do you mean the road is out? You mean washed out?"

"You'd have to drive around," the portly man said. "Thirty miles before you get to the expressway, and in this weather it would not be wise."

"I'm sorry, but who are you?"

The man put out a thick hand. Dark stubble colored his cheeks. "I am Heinrich. I own this establishment...along with my wife, Emma. And I think you may want to have your car looked at. The damage isn't inconsequential."

"That's why I think maybe it was a deer, but..." I noticed the eyes of nearly everyone in the bar quickly glance at each other before refocusing on me. I was fading again and I wondered if perhaps I had a concussion. Maybe driving wasn't the best thing at that moment.

I remembered the clump of hair I'd found in the car grill and pulled it from my pocket. Apparently I'd dropped the second clump I'd found on the barbed wire. When I held it up, several people stepped back from the table. "I found this in the grill of my car. It doesn't look like hair from a deer. Do these woods have any wild animals?"

"Wild animals?" Emma said. "What do you mean?"

"I heard something in the grass…saw something…"

"What was it?" Emma asked.

"I don't know. It was a growling, maybe a dog or…" I was struggling to find the word. "A wolf," I said finally. "Or a mountain lion, perhaps."

Again I noticed the eye glances. "There are no wolves or… mountain lions in the Black Forest," Heinrich said, taking the clump of hair and examining it before slipping it into a kangaroo pouch of his apron.

I looked to the man whose car had hit me. "You didn't see anything behind me? Nothing chasing after me?"

"Nothing," Ernst said.

I suppose it could have been my imagination, running wild in the darkness and the rain. Maybe the noise had simply been branches rubbing against one another and the moaning the wind through the forest. Except I hadn't just heard something growling. I'd seen the grass being trampled as whatever it was came quickly through it, toward me. I looked to the others, about to try to explain, but I could tell from the expressions on their faces that they weren't interested in hearing anything more about it, at least not this night. "Is there someplace close by that I could spend the night? A hotel, perhaps?"

"There are rooms upstairs," Emma said.

"A hotel would be fine," I said, getting a weird vibe from those in the room and deciding it best to move on. "I don't want to be a bother."

"You don't want to go out tonight," Emma said. She then quickly added. "We've already put your things in your room."

This gave me pause. "You grabbed my bag from the car?" I asked.

"I told Ernst to do so," Emma said. "Before your things were towed away along with the car."

"Towed?" I stood up and wished I hadn't. I felt lightheaded and dizzy. I dropped back into the chair. "Who towed my car?"

"The tow service," Emma said.

This was quickly going from bad to worse. "Why did the tow service tow my car?"

"You couldn't very well have driven it," Heinrich said. "Not in the condition you were in."

That, of course, was true. Practical. Damn Germans. "How do I get it back?"

"You can call the tow service Monday morning," Emma said.

"Monday morning?"

"It will be closed tomorrow, Sunday."

I wasn't going to wait that long. I figured I could call the rental car company. I patted the pockets of my jacket, then my pants. "My cellphone," I said to Ernst. "I had it in my hand when you hit me with your car."

Ernst shook his head.

"We can look for it in the morning," Emma said. "Come now, Mr. Quinn, and I'll show you to your room."

Hearing my name gave me further pause. Up to this point, I was certain I hadn't mentioned it. Slowly, so as not to make a scene, or to look ungrateful, I reached and felt my back pocket. At least my wallet was there. "How did you know my last name?" I asked.

"It's on the tag on your suitcase," Emma said. "Richard Quinn."

It was indeed. Anna and I had purchased matching suitcases for our trip.

"You sure you won't have anything to eat," Emma asked again.

I couldn't recall when I had last eaten, but if I had once had an appetite, I'd lost it.

The room upstairs was comfortable, even cozy, warmed by wood crackling in a cast iron stove in the fireplace. I could hear the rain beating on what I presumed to be tile shingles. Someone, probably Emma, had pulled down the corner of the sheet and the patchwork quilt on the wrought iron bed. My suitcase was at the foot.

"We serve breakfast until ten," Emma said. She pointed to a small table on which I noted a pitcher of water and two glasses and a coffee maker on a table beneath an arched window. "You can make coffee or tea here in your room. The bathroom is just down the hall. Do you need anything?"

"No," I said. "I'm fine. Thank you."

Emma nodded and stepped from the room, closing the door. When her footsteps faded down the hall I walked to the door and turned an old-fashioned skeleton key, locking it, and slipped the key in the front pocket of my pants. I lifted my bag onto the bed, about to open it when something made me look back to the door. I shoved the wooden chair under the doorknob.

I startled awake. The room had cooled though I remained warm beneath the covers. Light leaked through blinds covering the small arched window. Instinctively, I reached for my phone on the bedside table then remembered it wasn't there. I'd have to go back to where I'd been hit and look for it, or find a store where I could buy another.

I checked a cuckoo clock on the wall and noted that it was after ten in the morning. I'd slept nearly thirteen hours. Five or six was my norm. It could have been the jetlag, I suppose, or maybe I had a concussion. I sat up and felt pangs of hunger, along with a lot of pangs of discomfort. I recalled Emma stating that breakfast was only until 10 a.m. I got out of bed and immediately felt discomfort in my lower back, my right elbow, which I assume struck the ground, and the back of my head, which I knew from the lump had hit the pavement. I took a few deep breaths to get my bearings, grabbed my shaving kit, and walked gingerly to the table with the pitcher of water and glasses. I downed two Aleve and a cup of water and looked out the window. It provided a view into a yard behind the pub and inn that extended to the forest. There was equipment in the yard, a tractor and some other contraption. Both looked rusted and unused. I also noticed a garden with a trellis covered in vines. Just beyond it was a small wooden shed. The door, which looked heavily reinforced, sat at an odd angle, as if it had been blown off its hinges. About to look away, I noticed a woman emerge from the trees, walking through the grass toward the building. She looked to be about my age, mid-to-late twenties with blondish-brown hair. She was limping, favoring her right leg and when she neared I noted rips in her blue-jeans, along the thighs and at the knees. Though Anna had purchased pants brand new with the same look, these appeared to have been torn and muddied, or bloodied.

The woman stopped and looked up at the window with a gaze so intense it was as if she knew I was standing there, watching her. It caused me to step back. After a second or two I looked out again. The woman was gone.

I quickly showered, changed my clothes and made my way downstairs into the pub, expecting it to be largely empty. Instead I found the tables to once again be nearly full. As I entered the room the conversation silenced, glasses stopped in mid-air, and the clatter of utensils eased. Those at the tables eyed me with suspicion, or trepidation. I thought I noticed several of the same people I had seen the night before, but then I had been in no real shape to remember much of anything.

Someone hit the play button and movement and sound resumed. I took a seat at the far end of one of the tables, away from the others. Emma approached carrying a pot of coffee.

"You slept well?" she asked.

"I did," I said, though my body was stiff and my thoughts still a bit cloudy.

"How do you feel?"

"Like someone ran me over with a truck." Emma looked alarmed. I smiled and said, "I feel okay, a little sore, but okay."

I flipped over my white porcelain mug. Emma filled it. "Is there a phone I can use to call the rental car company?"

"You can use the phone in the house," she said. "I'll bring you eggs and sausage."

I sipped at my mug, the coffee rich and bursting with flavor. Eyeing the empty seat across the table, I thought again of Anna and wondered if she regretted her decision to leave me at the altar. I sat back when I saw a plate with two soft-boiled eggs, sausage and toast. I looked up, about to say "thank you," or "danke," to Emma but the words caught in my throat. The attractive blond woman I'd seen in the field held the plate.

"Thank you," I said.

She nodded, providing the hint of a smile and set down my breakfast. I was trying to formulate a question, something to ask her, but when she turned away I noticed what appeared to be fresh scrapes on her elbows, and the distinct limp in her step. I rubbed my elbow, which was sore from having hit the ground.

When I turned my attention back to my plate a man stood on the other side of the table, staring at me. Tall and strapping, with a silver crew cut, and the clearest blue eyes I had ever seen, he wore a long raincoat and carried an umbrella.

"You must be the guest from last evening," he said.

It was an interesting way to put it. "I guess you could say that."

He motioned to the bench across from me. "May I?"

I nodded and noticed that the clatter of plates and utensils had once again quieted. It seemed I had again managed to capture the attention of the room.

"I am Klaus Müller," he said, sitting and putting his cap on the table.

"Richard Quinn," I said.

"American?"

"Yes."

"What brings you here?" Müller asked.

"The weather," I said.

Müller looked uncertain.

"I'm kidding," I said. He didn't smile. "And why are you interested in me, Klaus Müller?"

"It seems you are a bit of a celebrity," he said.

"I highly doubt that. More like a speed bump." Again, not even the hint of a smile. Germans. "How did you hear that I was here?"

"It's a small town Mr. Quinn. Word travels fast."

"I haven't had much of a chance to look around the town. So tell me, what is being said about me."

"That you had an accident last evening in your car; that you hit something."

"An animal, I think. I didn't see it. It was dark, and raining. But based on the dent it left in my car, it was big."

"You seem uncertain."

"Not about the accident," I said. "I have the dent in my rental car to prove I hit something, and not a cat or a dog. My uncertainty is with respect to what I hit."

"You don't know."

"I don't. I pulled to the side of the road and went back to try to determine what I'd hit, but I didn't find anything, at least I didn't see anything."

"But you heard something."

I started at him across the table. His eyes bore into mine. If this had been a staring contest I would have surely lost. "Are you asking or telling me?"

"Asking."

Bullshit, but I went with it. "Yeah, I heard something."

"I wonder if you might describe what you heard."

"What I heard? It sounded like an animal growling and coming toward me."

"Coming toward you? Are you certain of this?"

"Well...the grass was..." I struggled to describe it. "There was something in the grass...something moving toward me."

"But you did not see it?"

"No. Like I said, it was in the grass. When I decided it best not to wait around to find out I turned away to run and got hit by a car."

"You were scared."

Not that I wanted to admit it but…"Yeah. I was scared. I don't know these woods. For all I knew it could have been a grizzly bear."

"There are no grizzly bears in Germany."

"Where were you last night?" I said.

Müller's face scrunched in confusion. "Was there anything else you saw or heard?"

I started to shake my head then recalled the hair. "I found a clump of hair in the grill of my car and in the barbed wire."

"You found hair," Müller said, his eyes widening. He sat forward, closing the distance between us. "Where is this hair?"

"The one from the grill of my car I gave it to the owner. Heinrich. The other one, I must have dropped when I got hit by the car…along with my phone."

"I wonder, Mr. Quinn, would you be willing to show me where exactly you hit this…animal?"

I gave this some thought before I answered. Finally, I said, "I guess so," thinking I could at least look for my phone while I was out there.

Müller drove a four-door BMW. The drive back along the winding road took just a few minutes. I was closer to the small town—stone and stucco buildings with a church at the epicenter—than I thought. The rain continued with no sign of abating anytime soon. The sky looked like November in Seattle, when the gray cloud layer felt like it was directly on top of you and the rain could persist for weeks.

"Here," I said, sensing as we came around a bend in the road that we were approaching the place where I had pulled my car over. "It was around here."

Müller pulled the BMW to the side of the road and handed me one of two umbrellas. We stepped from the car, popped the umbrellas, and I looked about. I walked down the road. "I must have hit it twenty or thirty feet back," I said, searching the edge of the road for my cellphone. I stopped walking. "I'd say right around here."

"You're certain?"

"No, but I pulled over just before the bend after I hit it...so."

Müller took a moment to search the road, but with the heavy rains it was unlikely any evidence would have remained. After a moment he said, "Where did you hear the animal growling?"

I looked about, saw the tall grass and walked toward it. "It was here," I said pointing to a still identifiable path in the grass. I stepped over the ditch, the water still running through it and climbed the slope to the barbed-wire fence. "There. You see where the grass has been pressed down but is starting to straighten." The path was not as pronounced as the night before but I could still see where the animal had traveled. "I saw something in the grass, coming toward me."

"Coming toward you? Not away?"

"Definitely coming toward me."

"A wounded deer would not come toward you," Müller mused.

I looked at him. "No. I don't imagine it would."

"Come." Müller led me back down the slope to the road. As we descended I again looked for my phone but did not see it. We walked back to his car and Müller opened the trunk. He considered my feet and handed me a pair of rubber boots. "Put these on. They may be large, but..."

"Why do I need these?"

"You will ruin your shoes," Müller said, slipping off his loafers and pulling on the rubber boots. Germans, I thought again. Practical and direct.

I removed my shoes, pulled on my boots, and followed

Müller back to the tall grass. He stepped into it and I followed, feeling my shoes sink a few inches in the moist ground. He ducked between the strands of barbed wire, clearly intending to follow the path in the grass. I followed.

"What are we looking for?" I asked, after a hundred yards of walking.

"I'll know when I find it," Müller said. He walked for a few more minutes then came to a sudden stop. He pointed, but as I was behind him I could not see what he was drawing my attention to. I stepped to the side and saw an area of flattened grass that looked very much like a place where a deer had bedded down for the night. It would have looked like such a place, except this bed was not empty. A calf lay there, or what had once been a calf. The poor animal looked to have been torn apart, with deep gashes along its body and across its throat. The carcass of the animal looked to have been eaten from the inside out and whatever had done the eating had meant business.

"That," Müller said.

"What could do such damage?"

"A local farmer, relatively new to the area, only about a year, has reported that something is killing his livestock at night. It is most peculiar."

"Peculiar how?"

"It happens but once a month." Müller turned to me. "So you see, I was most interested about your comment as to having hit something the other night."

"What kind of animal do you believe is responsible for the killings?"

Müller shrugged. "If I had to hazard a guess, I would say wolves."

"Heinrich said there are no wolves in Germany?"

"Heinrich is mistaken. Wolves are suspected to have migrated here from Poland and have been expanding their range, mostly in the eastern German region, but west and north as well.

There have been no sightings of any wolves in this area, but also no shortage of evidence, such as this, indicating their existence."

I gave this some thought. "So this farmer hired you to do what, exactly?"

"Find evidence of what is killing his cattle. The wolf population is larger than the government will admit, and without some proof, some evidence, the government will continue with, as they say in your country, their heads in the sand. If I can prove this man's livestock are being killed by wolves, he can recover compensation from the state. At present they refuse to accept wolves as the basis for his loss."

"What else could it be?"

Müller shrugged and slowly shook his head. "I am at a loss to explain further," he said.

"What will you do if you can prove it? In the United States wolves are protected."

"Here as well under Germany's tightly controlled forestry laws, but if I can catch one feeding on a farmer's livestock, I can kill it. Then I will have solid proof of their existence and my client will have grounds to recover compensation. I wonder if I might have a look at that tuft of hair you pulled from the grill or your car?"

I shook my head. "I told you, I gave it to the bar owner, Heinrich."

"Then I shall retrieve it when we return."

That, however, proved easier said than done.

"I don't have it," Heinrich said when we returned to the pub. "It was in the front pocket of my apron and, I am afraid, Emma washed it, as she does on Sundays."

Müller and I retreated to one of the long tables, nursing beers in two large steins.

"What will you do now?" I asked.

"I'm thinking, perhaps, to take the slaughter to the game."

"I don't follow. Do you mean bait the wolves? With what?"

"The carcass of that calf we located."

"Isn't that dangerous?"

"Wolves are, by their nature shy animals. They seek to avoid humans."

"Not the one I encountered."

"I wonder if perhaps that is because the animal was injured after you struck it. If so, such an animal would be far more dangerous to more than just livestock."

"When will you do this?"

"Tonight. While the kill remains fresh. Do you wish to participate?"

I gave this some thought. I didn't have a phone, or a car for that matter, at least not until the morning. I had another night to kill before the towing company opened Monday morning. Then again, I thought of the night before, of the growling as the blades of grass bent toward me. That wasn't exactly enticing. But, what the hell. I'd been left at the altar. Nothing could be worse than that. What really did I have to lose?

The rain stopped, but it looked to be just a momentary reprieve. I took the opportunity to wander outside in the garden behind the house where, I assumed, Heinrich and Emma obtained much of the herbs and spices and other ingredients in the food they served.

As I wandered I noted movement in a row of tomato plants and saw a head pop up above the vines—the blond woman I had seen that morning out my window and at breakfast. She was stunningly attractive, with strong German features and a lithe, muscular figure. Figuring it best to get back in the saddle sooner than later, I approached, determined to speak to her. Easier said than done. I came up behind the woman and scared her so badly she dropped the tomatoes and assortment of other vegetables she had collected.

"I'm sorry," I said, bending to help her retrieve the items. "I didn't mean to scare you."

She smiled wanly and said nothing.

"Do you speak English," I asked.

She nodded. "A little," she said and it sounded like LEE-TLE.

Up close she had Emma's sharp features—pronounced cheekbones, a thin nose and Heinrich's sharp clear blue eyes that, when she wasn't turning away from my gaze, were as clear as glaciers.

"You're Heinrich and Emma's daughter," I said.

"Yes," she said.

The picture was becoming clearer. "So you work here?"

"Yes."

"I saw you this morning, coming through the field. Do you live out that way?"

"No." She offered nothing else.

"You were limping and have scrapes on your arms. Are you all right?"

She looked away, picked up the basket and stood. "I must go," she said.

"I'm sorry, I didn't mean to—" I reached for the basket of vegetables. "Let me carry it for you," I said.

She relented, thought reluctantly, and we started toward the back door to the kitchen. She kept her head down, her gaze on the dirt.

"I don't know your name," I said.

"I am Mila," she said.

"Mila. That's a beautiful name," I said. "I am Richard Quinn."

"I know," she said.

I hoped she had asked Emma or Heinrich about the stranger, which caused me to wonder if Mila had asked Emma if she could serve me breakfast.

"You were hit with car," she said.

"Just a flesh wound," I said, trying out my best Monty Python.

It didn't garner a reaction. We reached the back door.

"Would you like to have dinner tonight?" I asked, throwing caution to the wind. When you've been left at the altar, a rejection to a dinner date was nothing.

"Tonight? No. Is not possible."

"Okay," I said, knowing I'd be leaving in the morning. "Well, it was nice to have met you Mila."

She stepped to the door and opened it. I stepped away but I did not hear the door shut. "You will stay here tonight?" she asked.

I turned, thinking perhaps her question would be an invite to, perhaps, a date some other night. Under the circumstances, I was game. "I don't have much choice. I'm waiting for my car."

"You will stay here," she said looking at me with sad, almost pleading eyes. The invitation to another date never came. She shut the door.

Müller arrived just before dark, picking me up outside the back of the pub, and explaining to me that wolves generally commenced hunting at dusk and were primarily nocturnal animals. "Like any hunter, they will return to a kill and feast on it until it is gone, rather than work to kill again."

"Why didn't they finish it last night?" I asked.

"Perhaps because you scared them away with your car," he said.

We parked up the road from the carcass. Müller donned a head lamp and handed me one as well, instructing me to turn the nob to determine if it worked, then to turn it off. I did so. He also handed me an army green poncho, though not the tourist kind that tore with the slightest pressure. These were thick plastic canvass he said would also help to camouflage us while we knelt in the grass.

I put mine over my head, adjusted the headlamp and proclaimed myself ready to go. For the moment, at least, it was not raining, though the angry clouds overhead made that a certainty at some point during our evening. Müller grabbed a shotgun from the trunk of his car, along with a box of bullets he shoved in the poncho pocket, and we set out.

We found the calf, which didn't appear to have been fed on any more than when we'd seen the carcass that morning. Müller, after several minutes considering the trees for the direction of the wind, found a spot downwind of the carcass so as not to give away our scent when the wolves returned to feast.

"Wolves are very bright," he whispered. "If they smell us, they will not come."

We found a spot in the grass and hunkered down, remaining quiet for what I hoped would not be a long evening. I hoped to get back to the inn in time to see Mila.

I don't know how long we waited, but sometime after the darkness descended over the Black Forest I said, "I can't see my hand in front of my face."

Müller looked up at the sky, which continued to cooperate. "A full moon," he said. "Though the clouds make it difficult to know this."

"Then how do you know it?" I asked.

"Because it is April the 19th. Last night and tonight the moon is full."

I gave that some thought and it triggered another thought, something Müller had said earlier. "You said that the farmer lost livestock once a month?"

"This is true."

"Why would that be the case? Why wouldn't the wolves hunt more than once a month?"

From the look Müller gave me it was apparent that he had not considered this. "I do not know."

Before I could question him further he raised a hand to shush me and in the silence I heard the low, guttural growl.

Müller heard it also, turning his head and looking to me for confirmation.

I nodded.

Müller raised up, but only until his head was above the tips of the grass. I mimicked the move but saw nothing. The growl, however, was unmistakable—coming from the near distance, perhaps twenty yards. I squinted against the darkness and saw the blades of grass falling forward, as if trampled under the approach of an invisible snake.

Müller dropped back down and I heard a click as he released the safety on his shotgun. Using hand signals, he told me to wait where I was, which really wasn't an issue, since I had no intention of following him. Müller dropped low and duck-walked forward until he'd disappeared into the grass.

I waited for the sound of the shotgun discharging. Seconds passed. Then a minute. And another. Beneath the poncho I felt my body sweating profusely. Lightening crackled, followed by the low rumble of approaching thunder. I looked back to where the grass had swallowed Müller, waiting for the sound of the rifle discharging.

Another bolt of lightning illuminated the sky, crackling just before the thunder detonated, loud and intense. I felt the first drops of rain, a pattering on the blades of grass and the leaves of the trees. It quickly intensified, as it had the night before.

What the hell was Müller doing?

I was about to stand when thunder again exploded, but this time I thought I'd heard the discharge of the shotgun. The discharge was followed by a horrific howling, a noise unlike any I have ever heard before or since. It sounded almost human. That sound was followed by an even more intense, and clearly human sound of a man screaming.

Müller.

My heart pounded. I felt my knees go weak as I lifted up. In the darkness I saw a hooded figure, Müller I presumed, running toward me through the grass. Behind him, the blades flattened, as they had the night before and as with the night before, this predator was not running away from Müller. It was pursuing.

The blades of grass parted and Müller stepped from the grass with a look of horror, but just as quickly stopped running, as if he'd suddenly frozen in mid-step. He stood there, for what seemed like seconds but was surely only an instant, before being jerked violently backward, as if by a string, and swallowed by the grass.

Something fell from Müeller's outstretched hand just before he disappeared. The shotgun.

The screaming was horrific, this time mixed with the guttural growling—the sounds of something feasting, tearing at flesh.

I rushed forward, dropping to the grass blind in the darkness. I felt the stock and picked up the gun. I cracked open the barrel. I'd heard only a single shot. One remained.

I snapped the shotgun closed and moved forward, into the grass, following the sound of the growling—the screaming had been silenced. The rain—coming now in pellets, nearly blinded me. As I stepped from the grass, I realized I'd reached the bed where we'd found the carcass. In it, I saw a single, large shape, an animal of some kind, but certainly not a wolf. This animal stood on its back legs, like a bear.

It heard or smelled me and turned its head, revealing two luminous red eyes each as large as saucers. Then it threw back its head and howled something inhuman and awful.

Panicked, I froze, uncertain what to do. The animal dropped to all fours and bounded toward me in two long strides. Instinct kicked in. I managed to lower the barrel and pull the trigger. The stock of the shotgun kicked at my shoulder, nearly knocking me down, and the violent recoil of the barrel caused me to drop the weapon.

The beast whined and howled. The pellets had found their

mark. I retreated, turning to run when I felt the tug on the canvas poncho and heard the fabric tearing. The beast had managed to grab the material with an outstretched paw. A burning sensation seared across my forearm but I managed to wiggle free from the poncho and stumble backward. I turned and ran for the road, willing myself not to look back for fear I'd lose my balance and fall.

After a brief reprieve, I heard the growling behind me, getting closer, as well as labored breathing. I'd hit the animal. I was certain I had wounded it. How badly, I did not know, though not badly enough to keep it from pursuing.

I could see the black outline of the road ten yards ahead. Fear pushed my legs to run faster. I burst from the lawn, stumbled on the uneven surface but kept my balance, righted and resumed running for Müller's BMW. I heard something come out of the grass behind me and this time I could not resist the temptation to look back. The red eyes glowed, though they appeared to be falling behind. Then, just as suddenly, they disappeared altogether.

I turned forward and saw Müller's BMW along the side of the road, my refuge.

I focused on it, hoping the car would be unlocked. As I neared, I again looked behind me. I did not see the red eyes and I did not hear the animal's pursuit. When I looked back, just ten feet from the BMW, I caught a glimpse of darkness in my peripheral vision just before something hit me. I'd played football in high school and this felt very much like the worst that sport had to offer. The blow drove me backward several feet. I hit the ground along the side of the road and landed on my back.

The beast had pinned me to the ground. It rose up and howled that same inhuman, horrible howl then it lowered its head. It smelled horrible, a smell I also could not place. I felt the heat of its breath, spittle dripping from its jaws onto my face. It lowered its head until its nose was just inches from my face. I forced myself to open my eyes. It peered down at me, as if considering me, rotating its head to the left and slowly back to the right, sniffing much the way a dog would.

Headlights rounded the bend in the road. The beast rose up on its back legs and turned its head toward the approaching lights. It opened its jaws and howled, an echoing reverberation. Then it leapt from my chest, disappearing into the woods.

The pub remained full. I sat at one of the tables, a bandage around my forearm where the animal's claws had broken the skin, and a blanket around my shoulders. I stared into my mug of dark coffee on the table, only vaguely aware of the others in the room and of their whispered German.

I couldn't speak, could hardly move. My body shook uncontrollably, as if chilled to the very bone. Sensing the approach of someone, I raised my gaze from my cup of coffee. Heinrich stood with Emma and Ernst. They took seats on the bench across the table. "Do you have any recollection of what happened?"

Sensing the answer they wanted to hear, I shook my head. They turned and glanced at one another, before returning their attention to me.

"Nothing?" Heinrich said.

I lowered my eyes. "No," I managed, the word barely audible.

"Tomorrow your car will be ready," Heinrich said. "It would be best then for you to go."

I nodded.

"Until then, you will stay in the room upstairs."

Again I nodded.

"Do you need help getting up the stairs?" Emma asked.

"No," I said. I looked across the table at each of them, knowing that their eyes held more information about what I had witnessed, but that they would never reveal it.

With effort, I rose from the table. I looked at the faces of the others seated at the tables, all of them silent. I headed up the stairs exhausted but certain I would not sleep.

In the morning someone knocked on my door. I rose from the chair in which I had sat and opened it. Heinrich held the keys to my rental car. "It is downstairs. Do you need help with your things?"

"No," I said.

He nodded once, turned and left.

I grabbed my bag from the floor and made my way downstairs. The pub had emptied. Emma and Heinrich stood near the door. I paused when I reached it.

"What do I owe you?" I asked.

They shook their heads.

I nodded and I walked outside. The rain had stopped, though the morning remained a blustery gray landscape. I threw my bag in the back seat and pulled open the driver's side door. As I did, I looked across the hood. Mila emerged from the woods as she had the prior morning, walking slowly across the grass field. She stopped and looked at me, as if appraising someone she had never met. Then, slowly, she tilted her head to the left and back to the right. I felt a chill run through me.

I drove the four hours back to the Frankfurt Airport, this time careful to remain on the main road. I no longer felt like continuing with my aborted honeymoon. I wanted only to get home. I passed through security and customs and made my way toward my gate, finding a chair, collapsing into it, and waiting for my flight.

I heard a phone ring and looked about, but no one sat near me. I realized the ringing was coming from inside my bag. I unzipped and opened it. Inside, atop my folded clothes, was my cell phone. The case protecting it was nicked and the plastic covering it scratched and chipped. I pulled it from the bag and considered the name on the screen.

Anna.

I sighed and, for a brief moment, I contemplated taking her call then decided I wasn't up to it, not at that moment, maybe never. I clicked the button and silenced the ringer, contemplating whether I would call her back, whether I would give her another chance.

I probably would, I decided. I probably would give her the chance to explain what happened, or at least to apologize.

As I thought of her, I felt a discomfort beneath the bandages of my arm where the animal had torn my flesh. The wound burned, then began to itch, a good sign, I hoped, that the injury was healing.

I sat back and felt something else, something I had not felt in several days.

I was hungry, very, very hungry.

ABOUT THE EDITOR

USA TODAY bestselling author **SIMON WOOD** is a California transplant from England. He's a former competitive racecar driver, a licensed pilot, an endurance cyclist, an animal rescuer and an occasional PI. He shares his world with his American wife, Julie. Their lives are dominated by a longhaired dachshund and six cats. He's the Anthony Award-winning author of *Accidents Waiting to Happen*, *Paying the Piper*, *Terminated*, *Deceptive Practices* and the Aidy Westlake series. His latest book is *Saving Grace* and his book *The One That Got Away* is currently optioned for a movie adaptation. He also writes horror under the pen name of Simon Janus. Curious people can learn more at SimonWood.net.

ABOUT THE CONTRIBUTORS

STEVE BREWER writes books about crooks. His latest crime novel, *Cold Cuts*, is his 31st published book. His first novel, *Lonely Street*, was made into a 2009 movie, and *Bank Job* is currently in development in Hollywood. A former journalist, Brewer teaches part-time at the University of New Mexico. He and his family own Organic Books in Albuquerque, NM.

SUSANNA CALKINS writes the award-winning Lucy Campion historical mysteries set in 17th century London and the Speakeasy Murders set in 1920s Chicago. Her fiction has been nominated for the Mary Higgins Clark Award, the Agatha, the Bruce Alexander Historical Mystery (Lefty) and the Anthony, and was awarded a Sue Feder Historical Mystery Award (the Macavity). Born and raised in Philadelphia, she lives in the

Chicago area now, with her husband and two sons. Check out her website at SusannaCalkins.com.

Ex-Army, retired cop and former Scenes of Crime Officer **COLIN CAMPBELL** is the author of British crime novels, *Blue Knight White Cross,* and *Northern Ex,* and US thrillers *Jamaica Plain, Montecito Heights, Adobe Flats, Snake Pass, Beacon Hill* and *Shelter Cove.* His Jim Grant thrillers bring a rogue Yorkshire cop to America where culture clash and violence ensue. For more info visit CampbellFiction.com.

ANGEL LUIS COLÓN is the Derringer and Anthony Award shortlisted author of *Hell Chose Me,* the Blacky Jaguar novella series, the Fantine Park novella series, and dozens of short stories that have appeared in web and print publications like *Thuglit, Literary Orphans,* and *Great Jones Street.* He also hosts the podcast, *the bastard title.*

ROBERT DUGONI is the critically acclaimed *New York Times, Wall Street Journal,* and Amazon bestselling author of the Tracy Crosswhite Series, which has sold more than 4 million books worldwide. He is also the author of the bestselling David Sloane Series; the stand-alone novels *The 7th Canon, Damage Control,* and *The Extraordinary Life of Sam Hell,* for which he won an AudioFile Earphones Award for the narration; and the nonfiction exposé *The Cyanide Canary,* a *Washington Post* Best Book of the Year. He is the recipient of the Nancy Pearl Award for Fiction and the Friends of Mystery Spotted Owl Award for best novel set in the Pacific Northwest. He is a two-time finalist for the International Thriller Award, the Harper Lee Prize for Legal Fiction, the Silver Falchion Award for mystery, and the Mystery Writers of America Edgar Award. His books are sold in more than twenty-five countries and have been translated into more than two dozen languages. Visit his website at RobertDugoni.com.

ABOUT THE CONTRIBUTORS

PAUL FINCH is a former cop and journalist now turned bestselling crime and thriller writer, and is the author of the popular DS Mark 'Heck' Heckenburg and DC Lucy Clayburn novels. Paul first cut his literary teeth penning episodes of the British TV crime drama, *The Bill*, and has written extensively in horror, fantasy and science-fiction, including for Dr Who. However, he is probably best known for his crime/thriller novels, specifically the Heckenburg police-actioners, of which there are seven to date, and the Clayburn procedurals, of which there are two. The first three books in the Heck line achieved official bestseller status, the second being the fastest pre-ordered title in HarperCollins history, while the first Lucy Clayburn novel made the *Sunday Times* Top 10 list. The Heck series alone has accrued over 2,000 5-star reviews on Amazon. Paul is a native of Wigan, Lancashire (UK), where he still lives with his wife and business partner, Cathy.

CATRIONA MCPHERSON was born in Scotland and lived there until immigrating to the US in 2010. She is the multi-award-winning and best-selling author of historical detective novels, set in Scotland in the 1930s, and contemporary psychological thrillers, including the Edgar finalist *The Day She Died*. After eight years in northern California she wrote *Scot-Free*, opening the Last Ditch trilogy of comic mysteries that take a wry look at her new home. Catriona is a member of MWA and CWA and is a former national president of Sisters in Crime. CatrionaMcPherson.com.

TRAVIS RICHARDSON has been a finalist and nominee for the Macavity, Anthony, and Derringer short story awards. He has two novellas, *Lost in Clover* and *Keeping the Record*. His short story collection, *Bloodshot and Bruised*, came out in late 2018. He lives in Los Angeles with his wife and daughter. Find more at TSRichardson.com.

ABOUT THE CONTRIBUTORS

JOHNNY SHAW is the author of six novels, including the three books in the Jimmy Veeder Fiasco series and the Anthony Award-winning *Big Maria*.

JAY STRINGER was born in 1980, and he's not dead yet. He's English by birth and Scottish by choice. His work has been nominated for multiple awards, included two Anthonys, a Derringer, and the McIlvanney prize. His stand-up comedy has made at least three people laugh. Jay is dyslexic, and came to the written word as a second language, via comic books, music, and comedy. He writes dark comedies, crime fiction, and adventure stories. Jay won a gold medal in the Antwerp Olympics of 1920. He did not compete in the Helsinki Olympics of 1952, that was some other guy.

SAM WIEBE is the author of the Vancouver crime novels *Cut You Down*, *Invisible Dead*, and *Last of the Independents*, and the editor of the anthology *Vancouver Noir*. Wiebe's work has won an Arthur Ellis award and the Kobo Emerging Writers Prize, and been shortlisted for the Shamus Award and the City of Vancouver Book Award. His short stories have appeared in *Thuglit, Spinetingler*, and *subTerrain*, and he was the 2016 Vancouver Public Library Writer in Residence. SamWiebe.com

Down & Out Books

On the following pages are a few
more great titles from the
Down & Out Books publishing family.

For a complete list of books and to
sign up for our newsletter,
go to DownAndOutBooks.com.

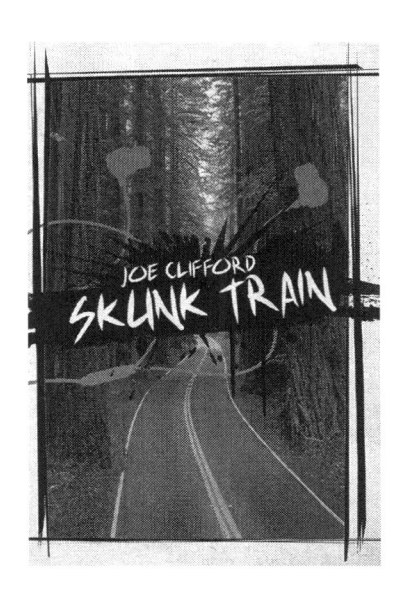

Skunk Train
Joe Clifford

Down & Out Books
December 2019
978-1-64396-055-5

Starting in the Humboldt wilds and ending on the Skid Row of Los Angeles, *Skunk Train* follows two teenagers, who stumble upon stolen drug money, with drug dealers, dirty cops, and the Mexican mob on their heels.

On a mission to find his father, Kyle heads to San Francisco, where he meets Lizzie Decker, a wealthy high school senior, whose father has just been arrested for embezzlement. Together, Kyle and Lizzie join forces, but are soon pursued by Jimmy, the two dirty cops, and the Mexican cartel, as a third detective closes in, attempting to tie loose threads and solve the Skunk Train murders.

Encrypting Maya
Lawrence Kelter

Down & Out Books
December 2019
978-1-64396-069-2

Encrypting Maya is the story of two exceptional kids who set out to change the world and a world that fought back every step of the way.

As Maya and Josh work to stem the tide of imminent global disaster, they face challenges both personal and professional and are beset upon by forces that seem to defy explanation—a shadowy figure drifts in and out of their lives over the course of decades causing irreparable damage, and the powers who once turned to them for help now seem to conspire against them.

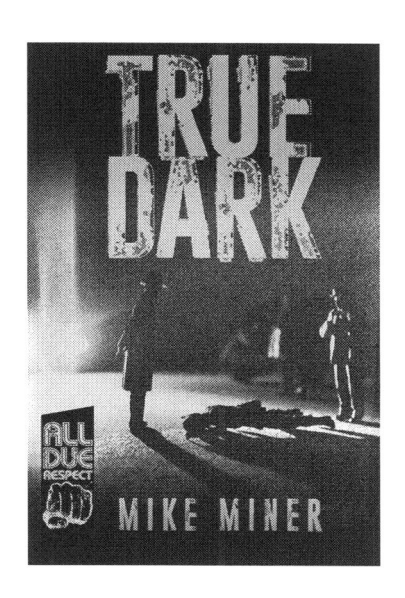

True Dark
Mike Miner

All Due Respect, an imprint of
Down & Out Books
November 2019
978-1-64396-045-6

Set in a tiny border town in eastern California, *True Dark* chronicles the trials and tribulations of the Murphy family.

Mike Miner captures a dangerous world where the lines between good and bad are blurry but the lines between family are black and white.

Kraj the Enforcer: Stories
Rusty Barnes

Shotgun Honey, an imprint of
Down & Out Books
October 2019
978-1-64396-059-3

Meet Kraj, low-level errand boy and hitman for Tricky Ricky Gutierrez. In upstate New York Kraj strongarms his way through the ranks of Ricky's shabby organization until he is ultimately committing murder for the man in charge.

Follow him in his adventures with his girlfriend Cami and night club manager Mikael on a trail of equal parts savage lechery and even more savage murder.

Made in the USA
Columbia, SC
19 August 2020